STOMPING GROUND

BY ERIC S BROWN

SEVEREDPRESS

STOMPING GROUND

WWW.SEVEREDPRESS.COM

ISBN: 978-1-923165-13-7

STOMPING GROUND

The wind was frigid. It howled through the trees making Adam pause to tighten up his parka. He'd known in Alaska it was going to be cold but this was ridiculous. His body just wasn't used to temperatures this extreme. Adam figured the windchill had to be below zero. He could see his breath in the early morning light. Everyone had told him and Walter that the winter was the best time to bag a moose up here but Adam was beginning to wonder if maybe they hadn't really thought this particular hunting trip through as well as they should have.

Adam gripped his .30-.06 tighter with his gloved hands, gritting his teeth, getting moving again in order to catch up to Walter. The fresh snow that had fallen overnight crunched beneath his heavy boots. There just wasn't any way to really be quiet up here. . .at least for him. Walter didn't seem to care about the noise they were making so Adam tried not to let it bother him either. Besides, there was a lot more to worry about. He and Walter were literally breaking the law. If they encountered a ranger out here, for all Adam knew, they could be facing jail time, as crazy as that sounded.

Walter was to blame for their lack of a local guide. He hadn't wanted some smug prick, as Walter put it, leading them around and getting in their way. No, Walter wanted an authentic hunting experience, just like the kind of trips they went on in the States. Adam had pointed out that Alaska was a state too but Walter only snorted at that and said, "Yeah but with A hole laws."

Adam couldn't argue that. Alaska law didn't seem fair to him either. The whole bit about not being allowed to hunt without being accompanied by a local just frustrated him. He knew how dangerous things could get, and quickly, in such deep wilderness and extreme weather but still. . . they were adults and knew how to handle themselves. They didn't need a babysitter to lead them around and make sure they were safe. Both of them were experienced hunters. To Walter, the law was more than just frustrating though, it was downright insulting. As thus, the two of them had decided to ignore the fragging thing and get on with finding some moose on their own.

So far, they'd managed not to freeze to death. Their first night had been as bitter cold as it was this morning. Breaking camp, he and Walter got on the move before dawn. The sun was just now fully rising. The area they were heading into was said to be heavily roamed by moose this time of year.

Walter refused to do any kind of still hunting, waiting on the moose in the area to wander by. Despite Adam's protests, Walter was determined they were going to find some tracks and use them to find their prey. The snow had stopped overnight so it was possible but their luck was apparently crap. They hadn't stumbled onto a single track yet. Adam wasn't holding his breath that their luck would change either. Something felt. . . off. During the night, the two of them heard noises in the woods, sounds of some creature that neither of them could identify. Walter swore that what they'd heard was a coyote but Adam didn't buy that. The cries were. . .well. . .there was an almost human edge to them, chilling Adam to his core. Sleep hadn't come to him easily and there was very little of it. He kept waking up to the sound of the cries, staring in the fire, keeping his rifle in his sleeping bag with him. The noises grew more distant towards the end of the night and finally could no longer be heard at all.

Adam looked around at the snow laden trees, eyes scanning for anything that might be a threat. There was nothing though. He and Walter appeared to be utterly alone in the cold. With a sigh that could be seen in frigid air, Adam increased his pace, catching up to Walter who had been a few steps ahead of him.

"You look like crap," Walter commented and then asked, "You okay?"

Nodding, Adam answered, "Didn't sleep much last night is all, not to mention it's cold as hell out here."

"Yeah, that it is," Walter snickered. "But when we bag a moose, man, it'll all have been worth it."

"You're only planning on bagging one?" Adam managed to quip.

Walter grinned. "Guess we'll see."

The two walked on in silence other than the sound of the snow crunching under their boots as the sun continued to come up. If it doing so affected the temperature at all, Adam was too cold to feel the difference.

The area of woods they were moving through was fairly dense. There was still plenty of room to move easily enough but the trees were much tighter together than they had been.

Walter suddenly came to a stop, his nose

wrinkling. "You smell that?"

Adam sure as hell did. The stench was putrid. The air stunk of rotten meat, stale blood, and a heavy animal musk.

"What the hell is that?" Adam asked.

"Frag if I know," Walter answered.

And those were the last words that Walter ever spoke. His head exploded like an over ripe melon as a massive, hair-covered fist came down on it with more force than a sledgehammer. Adam reeled backwards as chunks of Walter's brain matter and warm blood splattered onto him.

A roar that seemed to shake the trees themselves staggered Adam even more.

In front of Adam stood a hulking monster straight out of his darkest nightmares. The thing, though man shaped, was more beast than human. Its yellow eyes were filled with a burning primal fury. Standing over eight feet tall, the creature was all hair and muscle. . . a hell of a lot of muscle. Savage claws that gleamed in the sunlight tipped the fingers of its oversized hands. Adam gawked in horror at the thing for a fleeting second before whirling about to run away from it as fast as he could. Adam's legs pumped under him, his breath coming in ragged gasps. His mind tried desperately to process the insanity of it all. Walter was dead. Adam had just watched him die.

The monster that killed him, despite its size, had seemingly come out of nowhere. His best guess was that the monster had been hiding, somehow, behind the thick trunk of the tree that Walter was standing next to in the moment before he died. It should have been impossible for something so huge to sneak up on them in such a manner but neither of them saw or heard the thing before it struck.

Adam ran like hell. Glancing back over his shoulder, he saw the monster launch itself after him. The strides of its long legs were going to catch up to him in no time. He could already see that running wouldn't save him. Adam knew his only option that would give him any chance of survival was to turn and face the monster head on.

Zagging, Adam bounded around the trunk of a tree, trying to put some space between himself and the beast. It worked to a degree. With several yards between them, Adam jerked up his .30-.06, bracing it against his shoulder, as quickly as he could. The rifle cracked as he squeezed its trigger. The high-powered round it fired hammered into the hairy chest of the monster. Giving a half roar, half shriek at the pain, the monster stopped its mad charge just short of being able to reach him. The monster was shockingly very much still on its feet and in the fight. The round had hurt it but hadn't done anywhere near enough damage to take it down.

Adam worked the bolt of his rifle, struggling to chamber another round, but wasn't fast enough. The beast lunged forward again. A hair-covered hand slapped his .30-.06 out of his hands. The rifle spun away through the air. Cursing, Adam drew the large knife sheathed on his belt. He didn't carry a sidearm like Walter who kept a .44 Magnum holstered on his hip. . .not that it had done him any good. The blade was all Adam had. He sprang to meet the attacking creature. His knife sunk into the deep muscle of its left shoulder but not to the hilt. The muscle was so dense that the blade only made it halfway to its hilt before breaking. The blade snapped, half of it remaining in the meat of the monster's shoulder.

The monster drove a hand into Adam's abdomen, claws ripping into him. The red slicked, purple cords of his intestines poured out of the wound as the monster wrenched its hand free of his body. Wide eyed, Adam looked up into the monster's snarling face as its other hand swept through air. It caming smashing down, shattering Adam's cheek bones and jaws, driving his nose back into his skull. His body was flung backwards, sprawling out as loose strands of intestines flopped about like maddened snakes from the impact. A pool of red grew around his corpse as the monster reared back its head and gave another roar.

****

Two American Hunters Remain Missing, read the headline of an article on the screen of Ben's phone as he scrolled through his news feed. Ben stopped scrolling and looked up, peering out the window at the beauty of the scenery flashing by as the car barreled along the road. His driver, Martin, was really pushing to get them to Higton ahead of schedule. Martin had been with him as his personal assistant for a long time and as Ben saw things, he was a friend too. Very likely the only real one in his life. Having the level of money his grandfather had left him complicated things in terms of relationships. Ben was pushing thirty-five and was not only still single but very much a recluse, and a notorious one at that. The tabloids sure enjoyed speculating about why Ben stayed so much out of the world of parties and politics that his peers relished in. The truth was simple enough though the press would never understand it. He hated that crap. Ben had no use for all the drinking, drugs, heartless sex, and powerplays that such a lifestyle entailed. That was why he'd left the states proper and was moving here. Alaska offered a place far from the social traps and corruption of L.A. and New York. But there was more to his move here than just that. The land he'd purchased once belonged to the distant ancestors of his family. Reclaiming that land meant a lot to Ben. It gave him a feeling of pride.

The land was distant from civilization proper. The small town of Higton was the closest population center to it. It was there he planned to stay until his new home was finished. Construction had begun months ago but was still ongoing despite the steady stream of cash Ben kept pouring into it. Supposedly there was no problem with the land or the rather complicated plans for the house but something was certainly slowing things down and Ben wanted to know what. That was at least his excuse to rationalize his early arrival in Alaska when really it was because he was sick of his current life and longed to start a new one on his own terms away from the modern world.

"You okay back there?" Martin asked.

"Fine," Ben said more gruffly than he'd intended. Running a hand through his black hair, he sighed, seeing the look of concern on Martin's face reflected in the rearview mirror.

"You don't seem fine," Martin frowned.

Ben grunted. "Maybe that's true but I will be."

"No doubt of that, sir," Martin replied in a tone

that almost chided him.

"You know I need this, Martin," Ben shook his head.

"Didn't say you didn't," his driver smirked.

"I could point out that this was partly your idea, ya know?" Ben reminded him.

"Didn't say it wasn't," Martin continued on with his now playful banter.

"Oh frag it," Ben scowled. "How can any human being be so annoying?"

"Who said I was human?"

Ben knew the battle was lost, changing the subject. "How much farther is it?"

"Not long at all," Martin answered. "In fact, I'd say we're here."

The black Sedan turned into the parking lot of a quaint, small hotel.

"You're really a bastard, you know that?" Ben laughed.

"Just doing my best, sir," Martin's smirk had become a full out smile.

After the Sedan was parked near the hotel's front door, Martin came around and opened Ben's door.

"You really don't have to do that," Ben said.

"It helps me keep up appearances," Martin was still smiling.

Ben left Martin to get their bags and headed on

inside. A tiny bell above the door rang as he entered. There were no other customers in the lobby but a young, redheaded woman stood behind the front desk.

"Mr. Meyer," the woman beamed. "Welcome to Higton!"

Ben blinked, surprised that she knew who he was. It was the exact type of thing he had left the states proper to avoid running into.

"You know who I am?" Ben croaked.

"Of course, sir," the woman assured him. "Your people set everything up here in advance and besides, we don't get many guests this time of year and certainly not that drive up in cars like yours."

Ben shrugged, "I suppose not."

"I'm Kristen," she smiled. "This place belongs to my mom but I pretty much run it. If you need anything during your stay, just let me know. Now, do you need some help getting your bags up to your room?"

Ben shook his head, "No. I think we can manage."

"Oh, that's right," Kristen nodded. "We have a room for your assistant too. I'd forgotten for a moment you had someone traveling with you."

The bell behind him rang again as Martin came in carrying their bags.

"Ah. . .yes," Ben gestured at his friend. "This is

Martin."

Martin set down the bags to offer a hand to the young woman. Kristen accepted it and they shook.

"Welcome to Higton to you as well, Mr. Martin," Kristen said.

"My name's Greg. Greg Martin," he admitted. "Most people just call me Martin though. You do what you want."

"Okay, Greg," Kristen's smile grew a little wider on her lips. "I will."

Kristen handed the two of them the key cards to their rooms.

"Thank you," Greg said, meeting Kristen's eyes.

"Come on," Ben nodded towards the elevator. "Let's get going."

As soon as they were in it and the doors had slid closed, Ben burst into laughter.

"What the hell?" Ben teased. "Isn't she a little young for you?"

Martin threw him some shade.

"I'm not any older than you are," Martin huffed.

"That's my point," Ben said.

"This is payback for the car, isn't it?" Martin scowled.

"Maybe," Ben admitted.

The elevator pinged as it reached their floor. The hotel only had three floors so the ride up hadn't been a long one. Ben stepped out with

Martin following after him carrying their bags. The hall was empty. Kristen certainly wasn't kidding about this being the place's off season based on the lack of other patrons they'd seen so far.

They went into Ben's room first so that Martin could drop off his bags there. The room wasn't elaborate and he was fine with that. It was much like any other mom and pop style establishment. The place, while not fancy, definitely had heart. The room was decorated with a loving, simple touch. There were paintings that featured fields of snow, the night sky, and things of that ilk.

Martin set his bags on the bed. "Need anything else tonight?"

Ben shook his head. "Just don't stay up too late, Romeo. I want us on the road and to the construction site by dawn tomorrow."

"Roger that," Martin nodded. "Stay out of trouble. I'll see you in the morning."

Left alone, Ben plopped onto the edge of the bed, and began taking off his shoes. He was exhausted. He didn't care for long car trips but like Texas, Alaska was a large state. Hell, it was over double the size of the Lone Star state and the town of Higton was hours away from where their plane had landed.

Ben considered grabbing a shower before bed

but was just too tired to get up and make it happen. He got up and turned off the room's light, though some light from outside still managed to creep into the room around its closed curtains. Part of him was disgusted at how early it was to be going to bed but he finished undressing anyway, sliding into the bed. The covers felt like heaven, clean and soft. Ben fought to stay awake in order to go over the things that lay ahead in his head but was asleep almost as soon as he'd closed his eyes.

****

Henry took a deep, long drag from his cigarette then flung it down into the snow. He was angrier than Hell. Not only were things on the job continuing to fall behind schedule but now there was the local sheriff to deal with too. He'd stood watching the sheriff's car pull up to the edge of the clearing where Mr. Meyer's house was under construction. Of course it wasn't really a house. The thing was more akin to a mansion crossed with a fortress. Mr. Meyer himself was on the way to make sure the project got finished on time. Henry's reputation as a contractor was on the line and that was something he couldn't allow to be compromised.

Sheriff Hawk and one of his deputies were getting out of the patrol car as Henry approached it. It wasn't a good sign that the sheriff looked to have brought along backup. Sheriff Hawk had paid casual visits to the work site before. It was sort of a curiousity to the folks who lived in Higton, the closest town, and the site still fell within the sheriff's jurisdiction. He and Sheriff Hawk hadn't exactly hit it off but they hadn't really butted heads either. Their personalities just seemed to rub one another the wrong way.

After what happened earlier in the day, Henry had been left with no choice but to call the sheriff. A lot of weird crap went on around the construction site according to his people, and Henry had seen some of it himself, but until today, he'd been able to brush it all under the rug. Today, he'd lost two men, two good men, and that couldn't be hushed up or ignored.

"Evening, Henry," Sheriff Hawk greeted him.

"Sheriff," he said in reply.

"Heard you've had some trouble out here," Sheriff Hawk eyed him.

Henry nodded. "Come on. I'll take you to where it happened."

The sheriff and his deputy followed Henry across the construction site to its far side. There, Henry led them on into the woods beyond it. The sun was beginning to set but there was still enough light to see by. Henry's people had all stayed away from the area since the bodies were found.

"God in heaven," Henry heard the deputy mutter as they came into view of the grisly massacre. She sunk to one knee, turning her head sideways to wretch up her dinner.

Henry couldn't blame her for that. His reaction had been about the same when he'd first seen what was left of Aaron and Rollins. Even Sheriff Hawk appeared to be flustered by what they saw.

Rollins, the poor bastard, lay sprawled out on his back. There were deep, long slashes over his face that looked like claw marks. His eyes were wide, an expression of horror forever locked onto his rigid features. Rollins' ribcage was cracked open at his sternum. Something had savaged his innards, rummaging around inside of his chest. But as disturbing as Rollins' corpse was, at least it was intact. Aaron's wasn't. His torso lay several feet away from Rollins with only its left arm still attached to it. Of his right arm, there was no sign. It was simply gone. One of Aaron's legs rested against the trunk of a tree while the other was on the other side of Rollins. Aaron's head was near his torso but was utterly unrecognizable. Henry and his people had identified Aaron by the clothes on the pieces of his body, not the head. There was nothing that remained of the man's face but mangled flesh. Something had gnawed on Aaron's head as if it was an apple.

"What the hell happened to these guys?" the sheriff asked.

"How the frag should I know, Sheriff?" Henry snarled. "That's what I called you for."

"Some kind of animal attack?" the deputy ventured.

"We thought that too at first," Henry frowned, "but take a closer look at the ground."

"Holy mother," the deputy blurted out. "Are those. . .are those footprints?"

The prints in the snow were deep and far larger than any creature in the area, that Henry knew of anyway, could make. The creepy part was that they had the shape of a human-like foot, just a hell of a lot bigger.

"Yep," Sheriff Hawk grunted. "These are tracks alright."

He knelt to examine one of them closer.

"They can't be real though, can they?" the deputy asked.

"Are you suggesting someone murdered two of my workers just to set up some kind of hoax?" Henry challenged her.

"These ain't fake," Sheriff Hawk said, getting back to his feet. "I've seen tracks like this before."

"Then you want to tell me what the hell killed my people, Sheriff?" Henry demanded.

Sheriff Hawk turned to face him. Another man

might have balked under his glare but Henry was too angry to do anything other than stand his ground.

"I said I had seen their like before, Henry," Sheriff Hawk told him, "not that I knew what made them."

"Well you damn well better find out, Sheriff, and fast," Henry snarled. "This project is on a very tight timetable and I can't have it going to crap. Don't you even think about trying to shut us down, Sheriff. I'll have Mr. Meyer's lawyers all over you if you so much as try."

The sheriff just sighed. "I didn't say anything about shutting you down, Henry."

"Good!" Henry snapped. "Keep it that way."

"What were these guys doing out here anyway?" the sheriff asked.

"We're not one hundred percent on that," Henry frowned. "They might have heard something that drew them out here. A lot of weird crap has been happening around the site. For all we really know though, they could have just been sneaking off for a smoke break."

"Uh-huh," Sheriff Hawk grunted. "You wanna explain what you mean by a lot of weird crap?"

"Does it matter?" Henry retorted.

"It might," Sheriff Hawk fished around in the pocket of his coat, producing a cigarette and a lighter. Sheltering the end of the cigarette from the breeze with a cupped hand, he lit it up with the other.

"We can talk about that somewhere that we're not freezing our arses off," Henry pointed out.

"Yeah. Look, I am going to need you to keep your people out of this particular area until we get the bodies out and get some forensic work done," Sheriff Hawk glanced over at his deputy. "Go on back to the car and call this in, Mary. I want Jacob and Stevens up here pronto."

"Yes sir," the deputy, Mary, nodded and then scampered off, obviously happy being sent away from the carnage.

"I can keep my folks out of your way," Henry promised. "That's not a problem. And I hope we can both agree that this. . . this mess needs to be kept quiet."

"Yeah, Henry," Sheriff Hawk took another look at the bodies, "We can agree on that. Word getting out about this would just make things tougher for both of us."

Sheriff Hawk started back towards the construction site but Henry stopped him.

"Hold up," Henry said. "Is that it?

"What do you mean?" Sheriff Hawk frowned.

"I've got dozens of people not just working here but staying at the site too," Henry reminded him.

"Isn't your job to, I don't know, protect them?"

It was true. Henry had brought the bulk of his crew up to Alaska with him and the lot of them were living in temporary, shared trailers set up around the construction site. He was feeling responsible for any trouble they might be in but work wasn't going to stop regardless. The job had to be completed on time. That came ahead of everything else to Henry. Of course, keeping his people safe and getting the job done went together hand in hand.

Sheriff Hawk's head whipped about, eyes glaring at him. Henry wondered for a second if he'd pushed the man too far by the implied insult in his words.

"I have a town to protect too, Henry, and only so many deputies," Sheriff Hawk said. "There's no way I can give you the manpower needed to watch over an area as large as this construction site, not and do it right, anyway. My people will be up here tonight and in the morning retrieving these bodies and working the scene. At best, I can have one or two of them stick around after that if you want."

"One or two?" Henry stared at the sheriff. "That's it? People were killed out here, Sheriff."

"Two," Sheriff Hawk conceded. "Honestly, that's the best I can do though, unless you want me to call in *state.*"

Henry shook his head. "No. Don't do that. My boss would likely have my head if that happened."

"I may have to anyway," Sheriff Hawk confessed, "but I think we can handle this on our own for now. After we get the reports back on those bodies and know what we're up against in those woods, I want first crack at it."

****

Ben had forgotten to set an alarm but it didn't matter. While sleep claimed him quickly, it was far from restful. He tossed and turned during the night, haunted by nightmares that came out of nowhere. They made no sense to him. Sure, Ben felt some anxiety about the move north but that was normal for anyone striving to change the course of their life. And his dreams. . . they were nothing short of a wild horror show.

Rolling out of bed, he headed straight for the shower. The water brought him some peace as it flowed over him. Ben searched his mind for the source of the nightmares. Before leaving the States, he spent a lot of time researching the land of his distant ancestors. Ben recalled some of the legends, stories, and myths surrounding it. They had to be the source, as among them were tales of the Urayuli. The creatures were supposedly hairy, man-like beasts, often with glowing eyes. They were said to stand up to ten feet tall. The beasts were also known for their high-pitched wails. To Ben, the things were pretty much a bigger, scarier version of the Native American Sasquatch or Bigfoot. There was never any definitive proof of the beasts existing yet the anecdotal evidence in favor of it was massive. Ben read dozens of stories about the beasts from people who had seen the things from a distance or somehow managed to survive an encounter with them. The most distubring being of the town of Portlock. The people of the town were claimed to have had numerous nasty encounters with the Alaskan Bigfoot and ultimately driven out.

In his nightmares, Ben was standing in the woods, looking up at his new home. The massive mansion was finished and everything he hoped it would be. Its exterior lights pierced the darkness, illuminating the area around it. As he stood there, strange cries rang out in the night. Turning from the house, Ben saw numerous pairs of eyes staring at him from the trees. He sprinted for the house as an army of hairy giants burst from the trees, chasing after him. At that point, the nightmare would loop, again and again, always with snarling monsters gaining ground and closing in for the kill. Ben woke up before the beasts ever caught him, drenched in sweat and panting. That was all he could remember of the nightmares but it was enough to leave him feeling weary and on edge.

Stepping out of the shower, Ben dried off and tried to shove the remnants of the nightmares out of his mind, focusing on the day ahead. He dressed quickly and got ready to hit the road with Martin. While Higton was the closest town to where his new home was being built, it was still over an hour's drive to get there. His stomach rumbled. Ben pressed a hand on it. He couldn't remember the last time he had eaten anything. Picking up some breakfast, either from the hotel's lobby buffet or on the way, was going to be a must.

A knock sounded on his door. Ben walked over, expecting Martin to be on its other side, only to find the redhead, Kristen, standing there.

"Good morning," she said, holding a tray in her hands. "I know it's early but your man, Martin, told me that you appreciated your privacy so I thought I would bring some breakfast up to you."

On the tray was a plate of eggs, bacon, and a steaming pile of hashbrowns. Next to the plate on one side was a smaller one with a cut open biscuit and on the other were some packs of butter and ketchup. There was also an unopened can of Dr. Pepper which could only mean that Martin had a hand in her delivering the food to him.

"Thank you," Ben exclaimed sincerely, taking the tray from Kristen.

"No problem, Mr. Meyer," Kristen smiled. "If you need anything else, you know where to find me."

She turned to leave but stopped, glancing back at him to add, "Greg says he'll be along shortly."

Ben pushed the door closed in her wake with the side of his hip while keeping the tray steady. Taking a seat at the room's table, he tore into the food with a ravenous passion. Everything tasted just as good as it looked and smelled. Ben had cleared the tray in a matter of minutes. He sipped at what remained of his Dr. Pepper, leaning back in his chair, with a content grin. Just getting some food into his stomach had made him feel much better.

About five minutes later, there came another knock at the door to his room. This time, it was Martin, who was chipper and far more wide awake than Ben felt. While cheering him greatly, the heavy food Kristen had brought threatened to make him sleepy again.

"You ready?" Martin asked.

"As I will ever be," Ben shrugged.

"Didn't get much sleep, I take it?" Martin scanned the room, eyes seeming to be searching for anything that might have upset him during the night.

Ben ignored the question, waiting for Martin to

step aside so he could get out the door. Martin took the hint to drop the subject. The two of them headed downstairs. Kristen waved at them from the desk as they passed through the hotel lobby.

Martin slid into the driver's seat of the black Sedan as usual but Ben didn't get into the back. Instead, he got in up front, sitting next to Martin, who frowned at him.

"You must have had one hell of a night," Martin commented.

"Just drive," Ben brushed off his comment.

Cranking up, Martin guided the Sedan out of the parking lot and got them on the road to the construction site.

"So how did it go with Kristen?" Ben asked.

"Making progress," Martin wore a sly grin. "She's a nice girl."

"Uh huh," Ben teased, glad to have the tension between them broken.

"You might as well settle in," Martin warned, "we're in for quite a drive."

The bright morning sun stung Ben's eyes. Its reflection glaring on the white snow that covered the ground at the sides of the road made it worse. He slipped on a pair of designer sunglasses and got more comfortable in his seat.

It was lunch time before they turned onto the road that led up the mountain to where Ben's new home was being built. The road leading up to it was barely a road at all. The Sedan bounced along its loose gravel. Ben wondered for a moment if the Sedan was going to make it up to the site. Martin got them there though.

The Sedan pulled into the makeshift parking area below the shanty town where the workers were staying. Both Ben and Martin noticed the patrol car parked among the pick up trucks and other cars.

Martin gave him a look.

Ben shrugged. "No idea, but I think we certainly need to find out."

It had been awhile since Ben spoke to Henry, the site's foreman. He'd intentionally not informed him of the exact time they were arriving. Henry hadn't said anything about issues with the local authorities the last time they had spoken. Ben couldn't imagine that some kind of environmental protesters would be causing him trouble. The project was too hush hush for anyone but the locals and Henry's crew to even know about it.

Ben and Martin got out of the Sedan and walked up the small hill towards the site.

A burly worker noticed their approach and moved to intercept them. The man came bounding down the hill.

"Whoa, fellas!" the burly man shouted. "Where

y'all think you're going? This is private property."

"That so?" Martin stepped between Ben and the man. Ben hadn't hired Martin for just his driving skills. He also acted as a bodyguard when the need arose. He had served in the Sandbox during his tour of duty and done some mercenary work before signing up with him. Martin didn't like to talk about any of that stuff and Ben respected that, never asking too much about it all.

"Yeah, it is, buddy," the man snarled. His sandy blonde hair stuck out from beneath the construction helmet he wore.

Heny appeared at the top of the hill.

"Bruce!" he bellowed. "What the hell are you doing?"

Taken aback by the ferocity and anger in Henry's voice, Bruce went pale.

"Boss, these guys were. . ." Bruce started.

"Just shut up, Bruce," Henry barked and then pointed at Ben. "Do you know who that is?"

Bruce looked closer as Ben removed his sunglasses.

"Oh frag me," Bruce muttered, "I am so sorry, Mr. Meyer! I didn't realize it was you, sir!"

Ben brushed aside the apology and looked at Henry. His expression was not a happy one.

Bruce swallowed hard. The foreman had known he was coming but Ben figured their arrival came earlier than expected.

"Why is there a patrol car here?" Martin asked, getting straight to business.

"Oh. . .um. . . .We've had a few odd happenings around the site," Henry's clearly fake smile was rather sleazy. "It's nothing to worry about though. I've got it all under control and it's being sorted out as we speak."

"Sir?" Bruce balked at what the foreman said. "Aaron and Rollins. . ."

"Shush," Henry snapped at him. "I'm getting to that."

"Getting to what?" Ben cocked an eyebrow that showed his disapproval. If whatever Henry was leaving out was big enough for a worker like Bruce to comment on in front of him, it couldn't be good.

"We lost two men yesterday," Henry frowned. "Don't you worry though, sir. Their families have already been informed and will be taken care of. Now, if you'll follow me, I'd love to show you around the site. We've came a long way since the last batch of photos I sent."

"Hold up," Martin stopped Henry, not allowing the foremen to glide over what had been said and change the subject. "Was there an accident? What happened to the two men?"

Henry squirmed but answered Martin's

question. "No. No accident."

"Then what in the hell happened to them, Henry?" Martin pressed.

"That's rather a long story," Henry shrugged, frowning. "Are you sure that Mr. Meyer wouldn't like to see the site first before we get into all that?"

"Hell yeah, I'm sure. People are dead on your watch," Martin's anger and concern were only growing, not being assuaged by Henry's efforts.

"Henry," Ben cut in. "Martin's right. This is something that needs to be discussed. Now."

Shoulders slumping in defeat, Henry nodded. "We can talk in my trailer. It'll be warmer there."

Though the sun was shining, neither Ben nor Martin could argue that. The day was cold as was to be expected at this time of year in Alaska. As they followed after Henry, Bruce scurried away back to whatever he was doing before they arrived.

Henry's trailer was in the center of the temporary community surrounding the construction site. The foreman opened the door for them and Martin entered first. Ben assumed he was checking things out to make sure there were no surprises in store for them. Henry entered last, closing up the trailer.

The interior was well heated. It felt good. There was a work desk with a couple of chairs placed in front of it and a couple of filing cabinets.

Another door behind where Ben stood led into the rest of the trailer where Henry's private quarters were. This trailer was both his office and current home until the job was completed. Ben removed his heavy coat and hung it on the back of one of the chairs. Martin kept his coat on, eyes continuing to take in everything around them.

Henry walked by them to take a seat behind the desk. Pushing back his seat, Henry opened a drawer in the desk. From it, he produced a bottle of Vodka and a trio of small glasses.

"Would you care for a drink, gentlemen?" Henry smiled, pouring a glass which he lifted up to offer them.

Ben shook his head.

Martin accepted the glass. Sniffing it, the vodka seemed to meet his approval. He took a sip from it, staring at Henry. "So, you were about to tell us what happened to the two men. . ."

There was almost the hint of a threat in Martin's tone.

Henry's head bobbed. "Of course, of course." The foreman swallowed down the contents of his own glass as if seeking courage from it before continuing. "Two of the men working here were killed yesterday."

Ben didn't care for how that was phrased.

"Are you saying. . ." Martin started, but Henry

held up a palm towards him.

"No, they weren't murdered," Henry flashed a wry grin. Leaning forward in his chair the foreman clasped his hands together atop the desk, looking at Ben. "From what we can tell at this point, they were attacked by some sort of animal."

"An animal?" Martin sounded very skeptical of Henry's assessment.

"The local sheriff agrees," Henry nodded, assuring them that he was telling the truth. "They were killed in the woods just beyond the site. What we don't know fully is why they were there. It could be they snuck off for a smoke break or maybe they heard something that drew them into the trees. There's just no way to know. Regardless, something tore them apart and. . ."

"And?" Ben asked.

"And ate them," Henry said. "Bits of them, anyway."

"Frag," Martin grunted.

"Have you had problems with the wildlife in this area?" Ben dropped into the chair his coat was hanging on. It felt good to sit down given how heavy the conversation had become. He knew that expecting anything else when death was involved would have been idiotic.

At first, Henry didn't answer. That alone spoke volumes.

"Henry?" Ben stared at the foreman.

"Well, not exactly," Henry said at last.

"What the hell does that mean?" Martin was beginning to fume.

Henry was sweating. "There've been some strange things happening."

"How about you elaborate on that," Ben ordered.

"I am not sure you're aware of this," Henry frowned, "but there are a lot of legends about these woods you're building in, sir. The locals in Higton were none too happy to find out these woods were being cleared."

Ben shook his head. "You're only clearing enough to build my house, Henry, not threatening the environment by setting it all ablaze or something."

"Don't you think I know that as well as you do?" Henry spat. "The people here, to say the least, we got off on the wrong foot with them so when things started happening around the site, I blamed them. I thought. . .I don't know what the hell I thought, that the native ones had cast a curse on us or something."

Martin was scowling but kept his mouth shut so that the foreman could continue.

"You see, we started hearing some freaky crap in the woods out here at night," Henry shook his head. "Knocking, I think they call it, something out there beating on the trunks of trees. Crazy shrieking too like you've never heard before in your life. Whatever was doing it sure as hell wasn't your run of the mill coyote or any other animal, I or anyone else on the crew ever heard of. But things got worse from there. Someone, or something, started messing with our equipment."

"Sabotaging it, you mean?" Martin asked.

"That's one way to put it," Henry nodded, "But I don't mean like putting sugar in gastanks or crap like that. I mean like things smashed and broken. From time to time, we'd find claw marks too."

"And what did you do about it all?" Ben watched Henry shifting nervously in his chair.

"I knew you didn't want any attention beyond what couldn't be avoided drawn to your new home, sir," Henry said, "so we tried to handle it ourselves. We set out traps, posted watches, did all we could, but nothing worked. Things still kept getting trashed despite our efforts and all we caught in the traps were small game."

"But you did call in the sheriff," Ben reminded him.

"Yes, sir, I did," Henry was beginning to go pale from the stress he was under. "He came out and took a look around. Said there wasn't a lot he could do. After collecting some evidence of the damage that had been done, suggesting some new traps we could use, and pretty much interrogating us all to make sure we weren't behind everything ourselves, he left. We rigged up the new traps and doubled our watches. Things seemed to settle down some then."

"Until yesterday," Martin huffed.

"Right," Henry sighed. "Until yesterday."

"And you called the sheriff again then," Ben stated.

"No other choice," Henry shrugged. "People were dead. The authorities had to be brought in."

"I imagine that went well," Ben commented dryly.

"He and his people removed the bodies and essentially wrote the entire mess off as an animal attack, or that was the impression I got," Henry told them. "I asked him for help up here again as I know whatever is going on is way beyond anything we can deal with on our own."

"Then the patrol car we saw. . ." Martin started.

"Is the singular deputy he sent to keep an eye on things until his people can figure out exactly what it is we're up against," Henry explained. "Deputy Sorrells is a tough woman. Don't get me wrong, sir. It's good to have her here but the site is so large and she can't be everywhere at once."

"I get that," Ben agreed.

"I assume you're still having your workers keep up a watch too," Martin interjected.

"Of course," Henry said. "After what happened to Rollins and Aaron, none of us can afford to take any chances out here. Everyone on the site is scared that whatever killed Rollins and Aaron is coming after them next."

"There's something else you're not telling us," Martin eyed Henry.

"Is there?" Ben pressed.

Henry sighed, "Yes sir. Ever since strange stuff started to happen around the site, we've been finding tracks in the snow and mud."

"What kind of tracks?" Martin asked.

"Hell if I know," Henry threw up his hands in frustration. "Nobody can identify them. Not even the sheriff and his people."

"What's the deal with these tracks?" Martin frowned. "I mean, somebody should be able to tell you what they belong to."

"Maybe they can and they're just keeping quiet," Henry sighed. "I might too in their place. These tracks. . . you see. . .they looked like a man's but they're huge. And the toes are off."

"Toes?" Ben cocked an eyebrow.

"The massive foot leaving them is a bare one," Henry told him.

"You're not saying. . ." Ben blinked in disbelief

and surprise.

"I don't know what I am saying," Henry admitted. "It's crazy to think that there might be something like Bigfoot out there but at this point. . . I honestly don't know what else it could be."

Martin looked Henry over and said, "I believe he's telling the truth."

"Why the hell wouldn't I be?" Henry hopped out of his chair.

Catching him by a shoulder, Martin slammed Henry back down into it. "That's quite enough."

Henry glared up at the former soldier but didn't say anything more.

"I can't believe we're actually talking about a rogue Bigfoot here," Ben commented.

"Rogue?" Henry spoke up again, pressing his luck to an extent. "No. This thing isn't rogue. All that garbage we hear back in the States about Bigfoot being a big, lovable giant who just wants to be left alone, that's crap. The people in Alaska will tell you the truth. If there really are Sasquatch, Hairy men, or whatever the hell you choose to call them, then the buggers are straight up killers and violent as hell."

"Hairy men?" Martin asked, slightly smirking.

"Some of the natives call them that," Henry answered.

"Doesn't matter," Ben glanced at Martin.

"Hairy men or not, there's something out there that needs to be dealt with and I don't think your men keeping up their watch shifts and a single deputy are going to cut it."

"Agreed," Martin nodded. "We're gonna need to do something."

"What?" Henry asked, looking at Ben first and then over at Martin.

"Henry, I want you to focus completely on getting my new home built. I'll handle whatever is out there in the woods," Ben promised. "You just leave that to me."

Ben and Martin left Henry alone in his trailer. Not even bothering to take a proper tour of the construction site or take any kind of real look at the progress that had been made, Ben headed straight for their car. Martin followed after him, scowling.

"I don't like this," Martin said. "Two people dead and the best story that guy has about it is that a monster in the woods killed them?"

"You said that you believed him," Ben reminded Martin.

"Doesn't mean I have to like it," the former soldier countered.

They got into the black Sedan and Martin cranked it up, turning on its heater.

Ben was thankful for that. A harsh wind had

begun to blow on their way to the car, chilling him to the core.

"I'm getting the feeling that you've already got a plan," Martin glanced over at him from the driver's seat.

"I do and you're not going to like it," Ben smiled.

"I figured," Martin managed a chuckle.

****

In less than two days, Martin had made the calls Ben wanted him to and help to deal with the mess at the construction site was arriving. The return drive to the closest airport took longer than getting things together had but Martin felt like the trip had to be made. He wanted to be there for Heather, Burke, and the others when they got off the private plane Ben hired to fly them in. Martin hadn't seen any of the "crew" in years. He wished their reunion was going to be under better circumstances but how they were coming together again now somehow felt appropriate.

The plane sat on the tarmac as Martin drove up to it. He hadn't brought the Sedan, leaving that for Ben in case it was needed. The Sedan would've been too small for the crew and their gear anyway. Instead, Martin had brought a van that Ben rented for him in Higton.

Heather and the rest of the squad were waiting

for him already. She was just as attractive as Martin remembered her. Tightly muscled, thin, she stood with her hands on hips. Heather's expression was as cold and hardened as ever. Next to her was Burke. He was so geeky looking that one would never guess how lethal the little man was. Half a foot shorter than Heather, wearing wide rimmed glasses, Burke's jet black hair was now streaked with gray. The little killer was by far the most skilled killer of the group and the most bloodthirsty too.

Along with the two of them were several other faces Martin knew and remembered well. Harry stood next to Burke, towering over the little man. A lithe man who moved with uncanny grace. Harry was the squad's modern version of a pistoleer. Even from where he was, Martin's keen eyes could see the polished white handles of the customized butts of the pistols holstered on Harry's hilts. A wry grin was plastered on Harry's lips. On the other side of Heather stood Liam and Oliver. Liam was a hulk of a man. Standing slightly over six feet tall, with the build of a professional wrestler, he was a man ready for some violence. Oliver wasn't nearly as dark in his skin tone or demeanor. It was impossible for Oliver to stand still for any amount of time. He was vibrating with boundless energy. His speciality being demolitions fit him well because Oliver himself looked like he could blow at any time.

"About time," Heather said as Martin got out of the van, opening its side door so they could all get in.

"Good to see you too," Martin smiled.

"I thought you'd gone straight," Oliver yipped, bouncing up to them before either Heather or Martin could say anything else.

"I did," Martin answered.

"Then what the hell are we doing here?" Liam's deep voice rumbled.

"Man has a point," Harry smirked, walking past them to toss a large black bag into the van.

"What are we doing here, Martin?" Heather challenged him as she slid the side door shut, the others having gotten in and loaded up.

"Get in and I'll brief you on the way," Martin told her.

Heather buckled up in the passenger seat as Martin cranked up and the van left the airport, heading north.

"You gonna clue us in or not, boss man?" Burke called out from the rear of the van.

Martin glanced over at Heather to see her staring at him.

"I wasn't lying about going straight," Martin told them all. "I'm a bodyguard and driver for Ben

Meyer now."

"The Ben Meyer?" Heather sucked in a breath, recognizing the name of the famously rich man.

Martin nodded. "He's a pretty reclusive guy. Doesn't like people. Anyway, he's having a new home built up here to get out of the States and away from the slimy social circles and press that keep hounding him."

"Uh huh," Heather said. "And he needs a squad of mercs for that?"

"Believe it or not, he does," Martin assured Heather. "People have died at the construction site. . . or I guess I should say have been killed there."

"By what? Violent environmentals? Angry locals that don't want him moving in?" Heather chuckled.

"I wish," Martin sighed. "We don't really know what killed them. Emphasis on what."

"I'm not sure I get what you're trying to tell us here, Martin," Heather glared at him.

"You're going to have a hard time believing what I am about to tell you, Heather," Martin warned, "but it's true."

"Martin. . ." Heather said.

They'd known each other for years, put their lives in each other's hands. There was a bond between them that even went beyond that. Still,

Martin was well aware just how crazy what he was about to say sounded. He swallowed and tried to get it over with.

"The two guys who were killed on the site were ripped to pieces," Martin paused and then added, "Not by anything human."

"So you're telling me you called us all the way up here to hunt down what, a bear, a pack of wolves?" Heather laughed out loud.

Martin shook his head. "No, Heather, I brought you guys up here to help me protect Meyer's construction site from something that might really be Bigfoot."

She stared at him, as if unsure what to say. It was clear that she could tell he was being deadly serious.

"I know how hard to believe that sounds but you know me, Heather," Martin went on. "The truth is, I don't know what's attacking the site but every shred of evidence points to it being Bigfoot. The local sheriff isn't doing crap about it and even with arming his crew and posting watches, the foreman hasn't been about to stop whatever is out there either. That's where we come in. Our job is to blow the hell out of anyone or anything that threatens the site and its crew."

"Frag me," Heather muttered. "You sure know how to pick 'em, don't you, Martin?"

He shrugged. "On the upside, the pay for you guys is gonna be double your going rate."

Heather lit up at that. "Well then, your monster in the woods is gonna regret it if the thing decides to pay the site another visit."

Oliver, who had been listening from the rear of the van, whooped, "Whooho! We're gonna be hunting freaking Bigfoot!"

Liam said nothing. The big man just sat across from Oliver, scowling.

Harry cocked an eyebrow. "That's fragged up, man."

"A paycheck is a paycheck," Burke commented, not seeming to care what it was they were going up against.

"Just imagine the traps I'm going to get to rig up!" Oliver beamed, softly clapping his hands together in front of his chest like an excited kid.

****

Back at the site, night was beginning to close in. The sun was sinking behind the distant mountains and the shadows among the trees growing darker and thicker. Ben stood on the small, makeshift porch of Henry's trailer looking around at the community of trailers. There was no one moving about outside of them. Everyone on the crew, except those assigned to watch positions around the site's perimeter, had already returned to their trailers and scattered RVs. Ben couldn't blame them. With all the weird crap they'd been dealing with and now two of their coworkers dead, it was better to be safe than sorry.

Martin had given him an earful for opting to stay at the site instead of returning to his hotel. He was rather angry about the matter. Ben refused to listen though. This place was about to be his new home and nothing was going to drive him from it. In the end, there wasn't a thing Martin could do but relent or risk pushing him to the point of getting fired. Martin knew him well enough to know when to back down and finally relented, accepting that Ben was going to do what he wanted, no matter what he said.

Ben didn't have anywhere to stay at the site so Henry agreed to take him in for the evening. Not that the foreman had a choice in the matter, knowing that it was Ben's money that was paying for everything out here. Still, Henry was being nice about it. Nice to the point of where it seemed like he was making an attempt at sucking up to him and that annoyed Ben.

Henry walked out of the trailer to stand behind him on the small porch area, lighting up a cigarette. Taking a deep drag from it, Henry blew smoke out of his nose and said, "If you're looking for whatever is out there, you're not going to see anything. No one ever does. . .except for maybe Aaron and Rollins, of course. No harm in looking though I guess as long as you don't mind freezing your butt off to do it."

A light snow was beginning to blow around the evening breeze. The temperature didn't feel bad to Ben as Henry was playing it out to be. He turned to face the foreman.

"Shouldn't your man be back soon?" Henry asked, referring to Martin.

"Soon," Ben answered. He could see that Henry was nervous about having hired mercs on what he had to think of as his site. Ben had been upfront with him over what he was doing once Martin was able to recruit his former military buddies who were still in the guns for hire trade.

"I'll feel a lot better when they get here," Henry commented, though his words were dripping with insincerity.

"I'm sure," Ben glanced up at the sky. "It's a pretty clear night for snow to be falling."

"Hah," Henry snorted. "This isn't snow. It's flurries at best. You'll know it when a real band of snow comes through."

Ben leaned onto the porch's thin railing. Being metal, he figured it was strong enough to support his weight. "I'll take your word for it," he responded to Henry, still mostly disinterested in what the foreman was saying.

The sun continued to set and the darkness in the site and woods beyond grew.

Somewhere to the south, a gun shot rang out. The sharp crack startled both of them. Ben nearly toppled over the railing he was leaning on while Henry flung his cigarette off the porch. Henry sprang into action, lunging for the short set of steps to the snow-covered ground below. Ben sucked in a breath, regaining his composure, and then ran after him. Henry was heading straight for where it sounded like the shot had come from. As he ran, the foreman drew a concealed .38 revolver from beneath his jacket. Ben cursed himself for not having a weapon. Martin had offered him a pistol before leaving but he'd refused to take it, figuring that nothing bad could happen to him inside Henry's trailer in the center of the shanty community. Of course, he wasn't in Henry's trailer now. He was rushing headlong into likely danger, playing hero, without anything to protect himself with.

He kept pace with Henry, sticking right on the foreman's heels. Lights were coming on in the trailers and RVs all around them. Voices were crying out, confused and alarmed. Henry didn't stop for them and neither did he. Another gun shot rang out followed by a thunderous roar unlike Ben had ever heard before in his life. It made the hairs on the back of his neck stand up straight and sent a chill running down his spine.

As they reached the construction site and passed through its lower edge, the woods there came into view. Ben skidded to a halt in the snow, barely able to stay on his feet in doing so. Henry kept charging right on towards the nightmarish scene ahead of them.

A man with a rifle braced against his shoulder fired the rifle he clutched again. The thing he was shooting at didn't even seem to notice as the bullet thudded into its left shoulder. It towered over the man, standing at least eight feet tall. Its eyes glowed a bright, rage-filled yellow. The beast moved on two legs like a man, closing the distance between itself and the man with seemingly impossible speed for something so large. An overly long, ape-like arm lashed out, swinging a hand with claws that gleamed in the last rays of the day's dying light. The man screamed as the clawed hand knocked his rifle from his grip. Only then did Ben notice that there was another man lying on the ground, stomach slashed open with intestines bulging out through his torn flesh.

Henry raised his .38 at the monster. That was really the best word that came to Ben's mind to describe the thing. The thing was like savage violence and primal rage personified into a living creature. The revolver barked in rapid succession as Henry did his best to drive the monster away from the man it was on the verge of getting its clawed hand on. The bullets, while not appearing to truly do any real damage to it, certainly got the monster's attention. It whirled about, charging through the snow towards the foreman. To Ben's surprise, Henry held his ground, switching to a two handed grip on the .38. Aiming carefully, Henry fired again, this time a single shot. It smacked into the monster's forehead. The round didn't get any better penetration than Henry's previous ones but the impact did stun the monster.

The man behind it had retrieved his rifle and rejoined the insane battle. His rifle spat a fourth shot as he fired it one handed. The bullet struck the monster in its back. Head swinging upwards towards the sky, the monster shrieked in pain.

"Get the hell out of there!" Henry yelled at the worker.

The man didn't need to be told twice, sprinting past the wailing monster.

Ben heard the voices of several men racing in their direction.

Henry was backing up away from the monster as the men reached their position. The monster took a look at the number of armed men approaching it and bolted into the woods it had come from. Some of the men started to go chasing after it. Henry stopped them.

"Let it go!" Henry shouted at the top of his lungs. "This fight is over! Running headlong into those trees is like asking to get your arse torn apart."

The men listened to him. They stood milling about, unsure what to do now as there was no longer anything to aim their weapons at.

The man who had survived the monster's attack came up to Henry.

"That thing. . ." he stammered, nearly completely hysterical, "it came out of nowhere. Daryl was dead before he was even able to get off a single shot."

"Settle down, Keith," Henry told him, reaching out to place a hand on his shoulder. "It's gone now."

Ben saw that Keith's hands was missing the thumb and its pointer finger was snapped hideously backwards. Henry had noticed it too.

"Come on, Keith," Henry told the worker. "We need to get you back to camp and get that treated."

"But what about Daryl?" Keith asked, glancing back at where his friend's corpse lay in a puddle of red.

Ben was still trying to catch his breath. Despite

having seen everything that happened with his own eyes, the rational part of his brain was having a difficult time processing it and accepting that it was real.

"Your buddy Daryl is dead," a woman's voice answered Keith's question.

Whipping his head up, Ben saw her. The name plate on her uniform, opposite her badge, read Sorrells. He put her age under thirty. Long black hair was pulled into a tight pony tail behind sharp, angry blue eyes. She was stunning. Ben had seen legions of attractive women in his day but this Deputy Sorrells, somehow, managed to take his breath away. There was just something about her pale skin under the starlight combined with how hard of a woman she looked to be.

"Deputy," Henry huffed. "Nice of you to show up."

"I was on the other side of the site when the gunfire started," she told him, unbothered by his snarky comment. "I got here as fast as I could."

Henry gave a dismissive shake of his head but didn't say anything more about it.

"What. . .What was that thing?" Ben stammered.

"I only got a glimpse of it," Deputy Sorrells said. "But I would wager that thing was a Tornit or Hairy man, or as you Americans might say, a

Bigfoot. I mean, it sure as hell wasn't a bear or some dumbass in a suit."

"Jesus help us," Ben whispered.

"You must be Meyer," Deputy Sorrells looked him over. "Bet you're regretting deciding to build out here now, eh?"

Her words made Ben draw himself up mentally. Any fear and shock drained instantly away, leaving a firm determination in their place. "No, Deputy, it doesn't. It just means that I've got more work to do than I thought."

"Ha," she smirked. "Is that so?"

Ben, Henry, Deputy Sorrells, and another worker helping along Keith, who was in a rather bad state of shock, all returned to the shanty community and headed for its med-trailer. The EMT on duty there, a man named Chip, opened its door to let them in.

Chip took one look at Keith and had the man helping him get him to one of the medical beds. The man got Keith laid down there before Henry promptly ordered him to get out.

Going to work on Keith's hand, Chip started sterilizing the wounds.

"There'll be a body coming too," Deputy Sorrells warned the EMT. "I'll need it kept here until I can get some folks out to collect it."

"Somebody died?" Chip blurted out.

"Somebody was killed," Henry corrected the EMT.

"I heard the gunfire but. . ." Chip wrapped bandages tight around Keith's hand.

"You're not in trouble, Chip," Henry assured him. "There's nothing you could have done even if you had been there."

Ben could see that Chip wanted a hell of a lot more in terms of an explanation.

"We don't really know what the thing was that attacked him and his buddy," Ben told him, "but whatever the thing was, it wasn't human."

Chip, seeing that he was serious, swallowed hard, and didn't ask anything more.

"Now you see what I've been dealing with," Henry said. "Something out there, lurking around, that you just don't know where, when, or even how it's going to come at you next."

"I'd say you're beyond just getting equipment wrecked at this point," Ben asserted.

"You were smart to call in the people you've got on the way," Henry admitted. "It's going to take people like them to stop this thing."

"What people?" Deputy Sorrells demanded.

Ben shot Henry a furious glare.

"This is private property, Deputy," Ben tried to be as diplomatic as he could, which he might not have been if she weren't so stunning. "I have every right to do what I feel I need to protect it, so long as no laws are broken."

He wanted to tell Sorrells that her presence was no longer required but couldn't bring himself to do it. Part of him wanted her hanging around, that was true, but also, beyond those personal feelings, doing so would likely bring the sheriff down on them. No local sheriff he'd ever heard of liked to have their authority challenged. For now at least, it was best on both fronts to allow Deputy Sorrells to remain on site.

She must have been able to tell what was going through his mind.

"I'll want to meet these people of yours when they arrive," Deputy Sorrells said. "I am sure Sheriff Hawk will too."

"That won't be a problem," Ben sighed. "Honestly, Deputy, I am not trying to cause you problems. I'm just trying to protect what's mine."

"I get that Mr. Meyer," Sorrells sighed, "but it's my job to make sure. . ."

Ben stopped her. "There are no laws protecting that thing out there, whatever the hell it is."

"While that's true. . ." Sorrells started again.

"Please, Deputy Sorrells, understand, all needed precautions are going to be taken. I plan on making a defensive stand, not sending some half cocked, armed hunting party of locals into those woods," Ben argued.

"I guess we'll see about that," she responded, keeping the scowl on her face to a minimum that Ben wasn't sure he would have been capable of in her place.

"Fair enough," Ben relented.

Henry had been watching and listening to their back and forth, keeping out of it.

"I've done all I can for him," Chip spoke up, gesturing at Keith. "I've sedated him for now. He should be okay though when the shock wears off, as long as he continues to take care of those wounds and get some rest. I'll be removing him from the work roster."

"I expected as much," Henry patted Chip on the shoulder. "Don't worry about it."

"You think that thing will come back tonight?" Chip asked.

Henry shook his head. "Nah, son. We hurt the bastard. Pretty sure it'll need some time to lick its wounds before attacking this site again."

"Let's hope that's the case," Deputy Sorrells remarked and started for the door. "If you'll excuse me, gentlemen, I've got to go make sure your workers don't shoot each other in the dark and one hell of a report to call in."

Ben watched her go.

"I told you she was tough," Henry said,

misreading his expression.

****

By the time Martin and his crew of hired mercs finally arrived, Ben had taken over Henry's trailer as sort of a makeshift command center. The foreman had been dispatched to help Deputy Sorrells keep order in the shanty community in the wake of the beast's attack. Martin heard all about it on the way in to the trailer. A worker named Brad had met them, relaying all of the night's events as he told Martin where Ben was waiting and showed the others to their temporary homes.

Martin could tell that Ben was fuming as he entered. Ben Meyer was a complex man. There was no doubt of that. Still, it was unlike him to be so upset over anything. Martin wished he could turn around and step right back out of the trailer but that wasn't in the cards for him.

"Everything okay, boss?" Martin asked, already knowing it wasn't.

His words startled Ben, making him slide back away from the desk he was sitting at.

"Martin!" Ben exclaimed, looked embarrassed, and then seemed to relax, taking a breath. "I'm glad you're here."

"I heard about what happened," Martin said. "Was it really a monster?"

"I don't think there's any other way to describe

the thing I saw out there, Martin," Ben sighed. "If I hadn't seen it with my own eyes, I'd never really believe it."

"Damn," Martin took a seat in one of the two chairs in front of the desk Ben sat behind. It was easy to see that Ben had seen something that freaked the hell out of him, whether it was really a monster or not. The former soldier could only take Ben at his word. Nothing else made sense, despite how insane accepting the existence of such a creature might be.

"The thing was huge, Martin," Ben told him, a hint of awe mated with fear in his eyes. "Everything happened so fast. . . but I am pretty sure it took multiple hits from rifles and handguns. It was as if the bullets couldn't get penetration through the thickness of its muscle. It was like there was no stopping the thing. It did give up the fight though and vanished back into the woods. Henry firmly believes that we scared the creature off but, Martin, I think the thing just didn't want to engage us out in the open like it was. . .as if the thing knew it might have a real fight on its hands and knew that withdrawing to strike again later was the best play it could make."

Martin blinked at that. "Are you saying the thing's intelligent?"

Ben appeared as if he didn't want to admit that

the beast was. "Maybe. Or maybe it's just animal cunning that I am blowing up into something more."

Shifting in his chair, Ben leaned back. "Regardless, we're going to have to kill the thing. That's the only way to know for sure the threat out here is brought to an end."

Martin whistled. "That's a tall order. . .even for my crew. These woods are that thing's home turf. We're the intruders. It knows the lay of the land and how to use it against us. I mean, how long has this thing been out here, without anyone ever bringing real proof of it to the world in this day and age of cell phones and the internet? There's a reason they crack jokes about Bigfoot being the master of hide and seek."

"What are you trying to tell me, Martin?" Ben flopped forward, the front legs of his chair thudding loudly onto the floor. "That your people can't handle this thing?"

"I didn't say that," Martin shook his head. "I didn't say that at all. I'm just saying, this isn't going to be an easy job even for folks as experienced and professional as the crew I called in. The fact that they aren't going to believe, not really, that the thing's real until they see it for themselves doesn't help either."

"I get that," Ben agreed, having just

experienced the exact situation himself.

"So how are we going to play this, boss?" Martin asked. "Are my crew and I going hunting or are we focusing on securing this site?"

"The latter for now," Ben scowled. "If we go after it and Deputy Sorrells gets wind of it, she'll bring the sheriff into this mess and it'll all get even worse."

"Could be we'll get lucky and nail the bastard when it strikes again," Martin tried to be optimistic.

"I just can't understand why this is happening," Ben's forehead was furrowed with thought lines. He steepled his fingers in front of him.

"That's easy," Martin laughed. "We've done something that's ticked that thing off."

"But what?" Ben shot back. "Is it really so simple as to be the fact that we're building here?"

"I don't buy the environmental crap," Martin commented, "and agree that isn't it."

"The locals, from what I can tell online, believe that this land is the creature's home. What you said about being intruders is spot on, still, whatever is stirring this monster to action has to go beyond that. This thing didn't just straight out attack the site and workers here. It tried to drive them away before resorting to that."

"You're talking about how it was trashing

equipment and trying to spook the workers by leaving dead animals around," Martin said. "Not to mention the creepy shrieking at night."

"Yep," Ben confirmed.

Martin raised a hand to rub at his cheeks, "Oh no."

Ben cocked an eyebrow.

"You've got that gleam in your eyes that usually means my life is about to take a bad turn," Martin frowned. "What did you just figure out?"

"Nothing," Ben smirked. "Not exactly."

"I ain't buying that," Martin stared across the desk at Ben.

"Okay," Ben admitted, "I might have thought of something. Let's suppose that this creature, whatever it is, could truly be intelligent."

"You did say it looked that way," Martin affirmed the theory.

"What if that beast has an emotional, perhaps even a religious, attachment to this land?" Ben proposed.

"If you make the assumption that this place is where the creature was born and maybe even home to its people, I am using that term loosely, then I'd agree that such an attachment was possible." Martin got up out of his seat to pace and let out the nervous energy growing inside of him.

"Right," Ben nodded. "As thus, we might just

have a means of ensuring that the beast not only comes back but to a spot and at a time of our choosing. There is a last crop of trees left on the site that were meant to be a part of the scenery after the house is completed. I imagine if we were to, say, set them on fire, the beast would be driven to such fury that it would come running."

"Whoa," Martin blurted out. "That's a damn big leap you're making."

Martin stopped himself and thought for a second, "But it could work though. . .if you're right about the thing's attachment to this place."

"If I am right. . ." Ben let the words linger so that Martin could finish his thought.

"Then we'll need to be ready for that thing when it shows up," the hint of a feral grin beginning on his lips, "Make sure it doesn't have any chance at getting away before we send its hairy arse back to whatever nightmarish hell it crawled out of."

"That's your department," Ben smiled. "I feel confident that you'll have no issues arranging such a trap."

"Consider me on it," Martin started for the door.

****

The remainder of the night passed uneventfully aside from the sheriff and a pair of coroners from Higton picking up the body of Daryl, the latest worker to be killed by the beast. Martin was glad of it. The long drive of the day followed by the insanity at the construction site had taken its toll on him. Martin had briefly given his crew an idea of what Ben was planning for dealing with the monster and then turned in. Sleep came quickly and amazingly, he slept like a baby.

Martin's alarm went off just before dawn. The sky was still dark outside his window as the big man forced himself up and out of bed, his feet thudding onto the cold floor of the trailer. The electric heat was on and blazing but utterly failing to keep the room warm. Martin stumbled to the bath to grab a quick shower. The cold of the water made him flinch as it struck his naked flesh. Martin nearly stumbled backwards from it, sucking in a harsh breath. He tried to adjust the water but ultimately gave up and just rushed through what he needed to do before getting out.

The damn place was even colder when you were dripping wet. Ruffling his hair with the towel he grabbed to dry it, Martin returned to the small bedroom to get dressed. There was a lot that needed to get done today for both him and his crew, the sooner he got started, the better.

Martin took a deep breath of frigid air, stepping out of his trailer as the first rays of the breaking dawn pierced the darkness from over the distant mountains. He didn't head for the two trailers that were serving as quarters for his crew, instead launching himself at a brisk pace towards the construction site. He'd left orders with Heather for her and the others to meet him at the patch of remaining trees this morning. He was pleased to see that Heather, Burke, Liam, Oliver, and Harry were all already waiting on him. What surprised him was that Deputy Sorrells was there too.

"Morning, Officer," Martin greeted her, walking up to the group.

Deputy Sorrells was holding a cup of steaming coffee.

It was Heather who answered him.

"The good deputy here thought she should check on us before heading home for the day," she said wryly. "I think she's worried we might be about to get into some trouble."

"Not us," Harry smirked.

"No way," Oliver grinned. "Never."

"Seems she doesn't approve of us hired gun type folks," Burke grunted.

Deputy Sorrells, to her credit, ignored them all, her focus on him. "It's Martin, right?"

"Yes ma'am," he confirmed. "What can I help you with?"

"Your friends here are packing some pretty impressive firepower, Martin," Deputy Sorrells pointed out. "I'm assuming you have all the proper paperwork for it."

"Of course," Martin smiled. "If you need it, I can have it sent over to the sheriff's office today."

Deputy Sorrells had to know that challenging them on such grounds was pointless. All of them were ex-military, Ben Meyer had the money to get away with just about anything he wanted, and they were in Alaska, not L.A. It seemed a weak play on her part which made Martin wonder what the deputy was really up to.

"Do that," she ordered. "You mind if I ask how you and your people here have decided to deal with the. . ."

"The Bigfoot?" Martin couldn't help but mess with the deputy a little.

"The animal," she said, as if correcting him.

"Don't worry, ma'am, my boss knows that you and yours don't want any armed mobs rushing out into the woods," Martin assured her. "We're not going to try to hunt the thing down. We'll be better securing this site in case it comes back here instead."

"That's good to hear," Deputy Sorrells sipped at her coffee, making Martin wish he had a cup himself.

Martin made a motion as if he were tipping a hat at her by pulling at the hood of his parka. Everyone was bundled up due to the cold. It had gotten worse since the day before, as if the winter season was doing its damnedest best to fight for dominance a little longer. The weather was supposed to warm up though. Martin had been keeping an eye on it since he and Ben arrived in Alaska. Today's cold was bizarre and fit with his luck.

Deputy Sorrells, having checked on what they were up to, headed out. Martin waited until she was out of earshot and then said, "That lady puts me on edge."

Heather eyed him with a disapproving expression.

Liam gave a grunt.

"She ain't bad to look at though," Harry winked.

Burke rolled his eyes at the gunfighter's comment.

"Martin, this plan," Oliver spoke up, getting everyone back on track, "are you sure there isn't a better option?"

"What?" Martin frowned, turning to the tech. "Why?"

"Well, if you look at the placement of the trees," Oliver started directing everyone's attention to the trees and various spots around them with his hands, "there certainly are great places to set up positions where we can create near perfect killzones for anything approaching those trees but if something were to go wrong, you see over there, and there, we'd be left utterly exposed on our flanks."

Martin saw what Oliver was trying to tell him but was dismissive of it. "Oliver, we're up against an animal, man, not armed killed squads. All we have to do is get the thing to come in towards the trees into one of those killzones you just pointed out and bang, job done, and you guys are paid, and going home."

"I'm surprised that deputy didn't come down harder on us over our weapons," Heather commented.

"She's smart enough to know that would have been pointless," Martin said. "The lady's got a good head on her shoulders."

"You don't care for her though," Heather cocked her head at him.

"What I don't care for is how the boss has got googly eyes for her," Martin sighed. "I can't remember the last time he fell for anyone but you know as well as I do how dangerous crap like that can be."

"Yeah," Heather looked sad, "I do."

"So the plan is really to burn those trees tonight and just hope that thing comes running when we do?" Harry asked.

"Pretty much," Martin fluffed off the gunfighter.

"I want everybody packing the most hard hitting firepower you brought with you. There's no point in screwing around with this creature. I want it taken down with as few shots as possible. That means no showing off, Harry. Do I make myself clear?"

"You got it, man," Harry assured him. "But I gotta tell you, I ain't cool with burning the trees."

"What the hell are you talking about?" Martin whirled on the gunfighter in surprise, staring at Harry. "You kill people for a living and you're telling me that setting fire to some trees bothers you?"

"I didn't say I wasn't going to be a part of it, Martin," Harry suddenly sounded dead serious. "I just don't think it's right. It's like asking for trouble."

"You afraid of Mother Nature or something?" Oliver scoffed.

"Watch your mouth," Harry sprang towards the geek, grabbing the front of Oliver's heavy coat. "Or I'll watch it for you."

"Whoa!" Heather shouted, launching herself at the two. She elbowed Harry away from Oliver, protecting him. "Back the frag off, Harry."

Harry threw up his hands in a gesture of surrender but everyone around him knew just how quick the pistols on his hips could come out.

"You just make sure he keeps his mouth shut about things we don't need to be messing with and I'm cool, boss," Harry told her.

"Damn," Martin muttered under his breath, shaking his head. Harry was really creeped out. That much was obvious to anyone who looked at him. It wasn't like the gunfighter. Martin could only wonder what had put him in such a state.

"You good, man?" Martin snarled at Harry.

The gunfighter nodded.

Harry turned around and walked away without another word. Martin let him go, knowing he'd be back.

The best Martin could figure out was that the openness of the land up here might be getting to the gunfighter. He'd heard of such things and Harry wasn't exactly the most stable guy anyway. Martin had to trust that Harry would be fine when the crap hit the fan.

Martin, Heather, and Oliver scoped out the locale around the trees more intensely while Liam and Burke stood watch. Oliver already had the positions that were best for them to set up in picked out in his head so that part of things went quickly. Heather wanted to make sure the workers weren't going to be in their way when everything went down and Martin agreed with her on that. They weren't going to need the additional guns.

They'd only create the risk of friendly fire frag-ups. Martin made a mental note to talk with Henry about keeping his men out of the construction site for the night. Oliver was already pushing to rig up explosives all over the paths that the creature might take as it came out of the woods at them. Heather was reluctant to let Oliver get too crazy on that front and Martin backed her up on that. Oliver's eyes got wide with excitement as he told them about all the ways he could blow up the trees and set them on fire. They had to push some restraint on the hyperactive demo expert in that regard too.

By lunch time, it was all settled and the plan fully formed and laid out. After a meal of sandwiches and canned drinks, Martin led his crew and some of the site's workers in getting what they had come up with ready.

****

Ben stood at the edge of the shanty community bordering the construction site, watching Martin and his crew. The hour of the day was growing late and the sun was on the verge of beginning its descent in the sky. Henry was next to him, puffing on a cigarette nervously. Ben waved a hand through the air, attempting to lessen the amount of second hand smoke coming his way.

"You really think this is going to work?" Henry

asked.

"I do," Ben nodded. "That thing out there, for whatever reason, cares about this place. Doing damage to it will almost certainly bring it running."

"We can always replant those trees," Henry commented. "Hell, we can have saplings brought in or fully grown ones if you dang well want. This shouldn't set us back at all."

"I'm not worried about that," Ben sighed, tired of the foreman's obsession with keeping the terms of the contract between them. "What matters is stopping that creature."

"Of course, of course," Henry's head bobbed, a fake smile plastered across his lips.

Henry flung the butt of his cigarette away and instantly lit up another. "Your man, Martin, wants all of my men locked down in their trailers tonight."

"Almost sounds as if you have an issue with that," Ben faced the foreman. "Do you?"

"Not at all," Henry answered hurriedly. "I think it's a great idea. It'll keep them out of harm's way and from messing with what your people have planned, too."

"That's good but. . ." Ben looked at Henry, watching him closely as he went on, "I have a plan of my own I am going to need some help with."

"And Martin doesn't know about this plan?" Henry sucked in a heavy drag from his cigarette.

"No, he doesn't," Ben's lips bent in a wry grin. "And I would be grateful for your help keeping it that way."

"Right," Henry blurted out, seemingly realizing that wasn't exactly the answer he was supposed to give, adding quickly, "I assure you, your man will hear nothing from myself or my crew."

The color had drained from Henry's cheeks and Ben knew it was from more than just the cold. As slimy as Henry might be, when it came to getting things done well and on time, the foreman was no fool. He was sharp enough to know that Martin was the sort of man one didn't cross if they wanted to continue breathing. Still, it was him that Henry had a contract with not the former soldier and it was him who would be answered to above all in the end.

"What do you have in mind, sir?" Henry asked.

"I have faith in Martin's ability to handle this creature," Ben began to explain his motive, "however, this situation is an unknown even for someone as well versed in combat and death as he is. Being a person who doesn't believe in leaving things to chance if they can be properly prepared for, I'd like to add an extra layer of precaution to the events that are to transpire this evening."

Henry waited with baited breath for Ben to go on, not daring to rush him.

"What I need from you, Henry, is a group of men who can be trusted," Ben said. “Not just with keeping their mouths shut but at following orders exactly to the letter as well.”

Henry didn’t ask why, instead simply asking, "How many?"

"I think eight, perhaps ten should suffice. Can you provide that number from those already here on site?" Ben asked.

"Shouldn't be an issue," Henry was calming down, color returning to his cheeks.

Ben's watch pinged. He glanced down at its face seeing a new notification there. The truck hauling in the "tools" he'd ordered for Henry's men had arrived on the road leading up to the shanty town.

"Good," Ben smiled. "Go gather them up and bring them to me. I've got some things to give them that they're going to need."

"Yes sir," Henry scurried off.

Left alone, Ben's thoughts were focused on what he was about to do. Martin wasn't going to be happy in regards to any of it . . . if he was forced to play his hand. Ben hoped it wouldn't come to that but it was better to be safe than sorry.

Looking at the screen of his watch, Ben scrolled

through the list of items aboard the delivery truck that awaited him. On it were two flamethrowers, an R.P.G., and a crate of AK-47s with their accompanying ammo. Usually he let Martin handle such dealings as the former soldier's connections were better and more trustworthy. That hadn't been possible this time around. Martin would've never agreed to arming any of the workers in such a manner let alone of his plan to use them as added insurance that the creature wouldn't be able to escape the fate it had brought upon itself by messing with the site.

The smell of Henry's smoke lingered in the air, somehow, despite the gentle breeze. It made Ben sneeze. He wiped at his nose, fanning a hand through the air hoping to chase away the last dregs of smoke, and then, double checking its position, turned about heading for where the delivery truck waited. Ben knew he would beat Henry and whoever the foreman rounded up there but didn't care. It would give him a chance to have the driver open up the crates and prepare the weapons for being handed out. He just hoped they would be enough. The creature bled, he'd seen that with his own eyes, but still an uneasy feeling of dread that he couldn't shake plagued him. The thing was extremely dangerous, he'd seen that too, and underestimating it wasn't a mistake Ben was going to allow himself to make.

Night was coming soon and everything had to be perfectly in place before Martin and his crew set things into motion.

****

Martin crouched, freezing his arse off, behind a pile of stacked up supply crates. Oliver was with him. Though Oliver had proved himself time and time again under fire, Martin wanted the tech by his side tonight. If the crap hit the fan, he was still their weakest link and Martin didn't want to lose anyone in bringing the monster down.

Across the site from where they were Heather and Burke signaled that everything was clear from their vantage point. Harry and Liam did the same from their position as well. The three groups surrounded the cove of trees that Oliver had rigged to blow when Martin gave the word.

Glancing at his watch, Martin saw that it was pushing midnight. The night sky was lit by stars and the moon was mostly full. In terms of light, they'd picked a great night. Oliver was as twitchy as ever, vibrating with energy like a kid getting ready to tear into their gifts on Christmas morning. There was a mad gleam in Oliver's eyes as he clutched the detonator in his hands, dying to use it.

The beast hadn't shown itself at all this evening. That wasn't abnormal according to what Martin knew about the thing from the site's workers who had been dealing with the thing for a few months. Taking in a breath that was so cold he shivered, Martin figured it was about time to get things going. They were only going to get one shot at this. It would either work or it wouldn't. Once Oliver hit the button on his detonator, the trees would be gone regardless.

"It is time?" Oliver asked, as if reading his mind.

Martin nodded, "Blow the trees."

Oliver stabbed the detonator button and the charges he'd placed among the trees blew. It was a spectacular thing to watch. Chunks of flaming wood spun into the air, being flung outward in every direction. They landed in the snow, hissing and smoking, most of them continuing to burn. The cove itself was a sea of fire. Flames leapt upwards, lighting up the night almost as bright as the noon day sun.

"Woohoo!" Oliver whooped, unable to keep quiet.

Martin spun on the tech, glaring at him.

Oliver shrunk beneath the fury of his glare.

"Sorry, man," Oliver whispered, holding a hand up in a gesture of apology.

The trees were burning. Martin sighed. All they could do now was wait to see if the monster showed. Raising his SA80 to brace the weapon against his shoulder, Martin looked through its scope at the distant trees. He couldn't see anything out there among the shadows.

Tapping the comm on in his ear, Martin asked, "Anybody got eyes on our buddy in the trees?"

"Not yet," Heather responded.

"Nada," Harry answered.

"Stay sharp," Martin ordered. "We don't want the thing slipping up on us."

Martin had expected the monster to come raging into the construction site in a furious rage at the destruction of the trees. The fact that it hadn't worried him. That meant they'd blown the trees for nothing or. . .the thing was as smart as Martin was afraid it might be.

An hour passed with nothing but a frigid wind rushing through the site. The cold was harsh and even through his parka, it was freezing Martin to the bone. Oliver didn't seem as affected by it as he was. The kid just had so much energy that it seemed to make him impervious to the wind chill. Martin wanted to call it and head back to somewhere a hell of a lot warmer. He couldn't though. They needed to wait out the night and give the monster every chance to make its move before giving up.

And just like that. . .everything went pear-shaped.

Gunfire erupted from Heather and Burke's position. M4 fire chattered, echoing across the construction site. An inhuman roar thundered in the night. Martin and Oliver watched as Heather and Burke abandoned their position, breaking cover, fleeing from a huge, hairy abomination that came chasing after them.

"Oh crap," Oliver muttered.

"Frag it!" Martin shouted in frustration and anger, leaping up from among the crates that hid him and Oliver to go running towards the rout that was taking place.

Martin saw that Liam and Harry were doing the same. They were all closing on the hulking beast. Harry's pistols left their holsters as he ran. They cracked in rapid succession, one then the other, over and over. Martin knew that Harry didn't miss. Nevertheless, the beast kept coming after Heather and Burke without so much as being slowed down.

Burke whirled about, suddenly standing his ground against the monster. His M4 blazed on full auto. A dozen rounds or more hammered into the monster's chest. It was still a juggernaut of primal fury though and despite the damage it was taking, plowed straight into Burke. The short man cried out as he was knocked from his feet and sent rolling through the snow, bones snapping and breaking inside of his body. The monster had to have hit him with something close to the force of a runaway eighteen wheeler. When his body came to a stop, it was clear that Burke was dead. His body was bent and twisted at utterly unnatural angles.

Martin jerked up his SA80, opening fire on the monster. A round dug into the flesh of its right shoulder. Another sliced a streak of red across the side of its neck. And several more punched into the right side of its abdomen. They got the monster's attention. Snarling, it altered the course of its charge, bounding through the snow at him.

"Watch out!" Heather shouted in warning.

Harry had skidded to a halt and was busy reloading his pistols.

Oliver was still cowering among the crates, having yet to join the battle.

Liam was the closest to him and the monster. The big man was armed with a pump action shotgun. It boomed as Liam sent a heavy slug plunging into the monster's already bloodied chest. The slug must have done some real damage as the monster staggered. Liam worked the pump of the shotgun, chambering another round. The wounds the monster had taken were adding up. Blood streamed out from where the shotgun slug had entered. Martin rushed forward, firing as he went.

His SA80 barked as Martin popped off shots into the monster. They were enough to bring the monster to its knees. Its fury was still unrelenting though. Eyes burning with rage, the monster looked at him as it unleashed another roar, spittle flying from its black lips. Martin met its rage with a battle cry of his own, roaring, as he emptied the remainder of his SA80's magazine into the monster's face. Hair-covered cheeks caved in as bullets crushed bone. The monster's nose was reduced to splattering gore. One eye was pulped in its socket, the other knocked loose to dangle by thin strands of sinew, flopping about wildly as the monster collapsed, toppling over sideways.

"Yeah!" Liam thrust a fist at the monster's corpse. "Choke on that, you fragger!"

Martin was slicked with sweat despite the cold. His breath was coming in ragged gasps, heart hammering against his ribs. He was staring at the monster's body, lost in the sight of the carnage he had wrought. It took all his willpower to calm himself and recenter his attention to where it needed to be. Martin looked around to see Liam walking towards Harry. Heather was kneeling next to Burke's broken and twisted corpse, confirming that he was indeed dead and beyond help.

The cove of trees continued to burn. Ash floated like snow in the flame lit air. Martin took a step closer to the monster's body. Though what was left of its face was little more than something akin to ground meat, the rest of it was still very much intact. It was creepy just how much the creature resembled a man in some ways, though it also made him think of an ape on steroids. Where the hell had the thing even come from? How did you even get a mutation of such nature? Was it the missing link between man and ape or something far more sinister? Martin knew he would never get the answers to any of those questions. This thing wasn't going to be taken out of here to be studied or even shown to the world at large. Ben had given strict orders to make sure the monster's corpse was destroyed because anything else would only lead to so much attention being drawn to the site that it would likely become a tourist attraction for decades to come.

The loss of Burke stung Martin badly. They were so careful in their planning, he'd hoped that no one would be hurt, much less killed. The monster hadn't played by the rules though. Death was a constant when you went into combat. There was no magical answer to keeping everyone on your side alive but damnit, he'd tried and thought that pulling it off tonight was possible.

Liam and Harry came over to where the monster's corpse lay in the snow.

"So that's what a Bigfoot looks like in real life?" Liam snorted. "Bugger wasn't that hard to kill."

Martin felt like yelling at Liam over that last bit with Burke lying dead not far away, but bit his tongue. There was no point adding anything else negative to the night.

"We gonna burn that thing here or just drag it over there?" Harry gestured at the burning cove of trees.

Liam shouldered his shotgun by its strap and knelt next to the Sasquatch body. Getting a firm grip on it, he tried to lift the beast.

"Ugh!" Liam heaved and barely managed to move the corpse. "This thing weighs a fragging ton! Ain't no way we're getting it over there without help."

"Whatever," Martin said. "Just get it done."

"I'll go get some gas to get it started with before Oliver tries using this for an excuse to rig up some more charges," Harry quipped with a wry grin.

Harry froze in his tracks as he started towards the shanty town as a chorus of inhuman shrieks rang out in the night.

"What the frag?" Liam rasped, swinging his shotgun from his shoulder back into his hands.

No, Martin thought, *it can't be. There can't be more than one.*

Heather leapt up from where she knelt next to

what was left of Burke. "We got incoming!"

Martin saw what she meant. Thudding noises filled the trees and were drawing closer with each passing second. They were the sound of heavy footfalls, had to be. "Everybody, form up on me!"

The small group raced to form a firing line facing the direction of the noise as a snarling Sasquatch burst out from among the trees into the flame lit area where they were. Behind it came another, then another, and still more. Martin counted seven of the monsters before yelling, "Take the bastards down!"

Liam's shotgun boomed, Harry's pistols cracked, and M4s blazed away on full auto as the group poured rounds into the charging beasts. A Sasquatch's eyes exploded in their sockets from a pair of well placed shots by Harry. Another stumbled and went down as a heavy shotgun slug shattered its right knee. The other Sasquatch kept coming, trampling the one that had fallen.

"Fall back!" Martin yelled, seeing that making a stand like he and the others were would only get them killed.

The small group of ex-soldiers separated, heading off at different angles of retreat. Oliver didn't move fast enough. Unintentionally left slightly behind, the tech had started to make a run for it only to have an oversized hair-covered hand clasp his shoulder. The Sasquatch yanked Oliver around to face it as the beast plunged its other hand into his abdomen. The beast's fist went all the way through Oliver, bursting out of his back in an explosion of blood. Oliver died instantly. Flinging his body aside, the Sasquatch rejoined the rest of its brothers and sisters in their pursuit of Martin and the others.

Liam was the next to die. Having caught sight of what was happening to Oliver, the big man stopped and turned back to try to help him. Liam had watched helplessly as the tech and demo expert died, unable to get a clear shot at the monster who was attacking him. There was no time to attempt to retreat again himself. The beasts were too close to him. Turning his back on them would only get him killed too. Opting to go out fighting, Liam blasted the closest Sasquatch. His shotgun thundered as he blew a gaping hole in the side of a Sasquatch's skull. The beast's eyes rolled up in their sockets as part of its brain was ripped from its head and then dropped like a rock onto the snow-covered ground. Working the pump of his shotgun, Liam chambered another round. As he took aim at another Sasquatch, one he didn't notice came at him from his left flank. The Sasquatch snatched the shotgun from Liam's grasp. It snapped the weapon in two like a twig and flung the pieces away. Liam yanked his sidearm from the holster on his hip. It was a .50 Desert Eagle. Squeezing the trigger of the pistol as fast as his finger could work it, Liam sent the beast that had taken his shotgun back to whatever hell had given birth to it. He'd learned to aim for the head of the Sasquatch creatures as they weren't protected by the super dense layers of muscles that made it difficult to hurt them if you put rounds into their torsos. The .50 rounds blew the Sasquatch's head apart, sending splashes of blood and fragments of brain matter spraying.

A Sasquatch charged into Liam like a linebacker before he could shift his aim to target it. It swept Liam up, lifting him from the snow, and took the big man to the ground, slamming him beneath its weight. Blood erupted from Liam's mouth like projectile vomit as his ribs broke, folding inwards, and his guts were squished.

****

Ben had watched Martin and his squad manage to kill the first beast. Seeing it dead made Ben smile. He stood hidden at the edge of where the construction site met the shanty town the workers were living in until the job was done. Around him were over half a dozen armed workers and Henry. One of the men carried an RPG, two wore flamethrowers on their backs, and the rest clutched

AK-47s, including Henry. Ben even had an AK-47 himself, though he had certainly never planned on actually using the weapon. Just before all hell broke loose, Ben was about to send the men with the flamethrowers to help Martin and his people dispose of the first Sasquatch's corpse.

Martin and his people hadn't known that he and the workers were gathered where they were as a secondary line against the monster which had now turned out to be monsters. They saw them now as they hauled arse to join their ranks.

"Cover them!" Ben heard his own voice shout in so much shock that he barely got the order out.

The worker with the RPG put the huge weapon to use. Its rocket launched towards the approaching wave of Sasquatch. The beast it struck exploded, limbs ripped off and sent spinning away in the night like shrapnel. The Sasquatch were still out of range of the flamethrowers but the workers with AK-47s let loose. A barrage of fully automatic rounds rained down on the Sasquatch.

Ben realized too late that the inexperienced workers weren't prepared to deal with Martin and his people being in their line of fire. Martin died as 7.62 bullets tore him to shreds. His run was brought to a halt as he jerked about like a puppet on the strings of an insane puppeteer. Heather and Harry flung themselves down onto the snow, dropping beneath the bullets that flew over them towards the beasts.

Unable to retract the order he'd given, Ben felt sick. The men he'd gathered up and armed had just killed his best and perhaps only real friend on the planet. And there was nothing he could do for Heather and Harry. The workers had to keep firing and do as much damage to the Sasquatch as possible before they closed in. . . and the Sasquatch were managing to close in despite the amount of rounds striking their ranks.

Henry's AK-47 fell into the snow as the foreman dropped it and whirled about to run like hell away from the battle. Ben saw and made a mental note to make the cowardly bastard pay if he survived long enough to do it.

As the Sasquatch drew closer, the men with the AK-47s, Ben included, stepped back so that the two with the flamethrowers could attempt to stop them. Twin geysers of fire shot into and over the beasts. The Sasquatch at the head of the charging pack shrieked and howled as the thick hair covering their bodies was set ablaze. Flesh cooked, fat bubbled, and eyeballs popped. Still, it wasn't enough. While the lead Sasquatch fell, those behind them separated in a V formation, coming in around the blasts of flames. The workers saw what was happening and the last bits of courage and discipline making them stand their ground died. They scattered, leaving the two with the flamethrowers on their own to be flanked by the monsters. Ben, hating himself for it, made a run for it too as there was nothing he could do on his own to save them.

The two men with the flamethrowers weren't going down without a fight though. They saw what was happening too. Jud broke left, Lewis right. Both hightailing it away from the approaching beasts. Jud didn't make it far. A beast bolted by him and positioned itself right in his path. Jud tried to skid to a halt but that was impossible on the frozen snow. He thudded into the beast. Its hairy arms closed around him. Jud screamed as the beast began to squeeze. His cry was silenced as the flamethrower blew from the pressure being exerted upon it. The blast lit the darkness like a mass of igniting fireworks. Flames shot upwards and outwards. The chemicals from the flamethrower continued to burn atop the snow-covered ground. Jud and the Sasquatch that had attacked him were simply gone as far as Ben could see.

In the shanty town that Ben and his men were making a run for, the workers were all waking up. The gunfire and explosions had shaken the night. A lot of men were emerging from their trailers and

RVs with whatever weapons they owned. Some only clutched large kitchen knives, others were packing shotguns or hunting rifles. Here and there Ben saw men with revolvers and pistols. Thank God for Alaska's looser gun laws. Maybe this wasn't about to turn into the flat out massacre it could have been somewhere else like L.A. These were working men, and armed. They weren't shying away from a fight when it came barreling down on them, instead the workers were getting ready to face it head on. Well, at least most of them. There were some trailers and RVs where the lights had come on but no one came out. Ben figured those men and women were doing what they could to get ready to protect themselves if the battle outside went to the beasts. That way, perhaps someone would survive to tell the story of what happened here at least. Of course, Ben couldn't allow that. As long as he made it through this hellish nightmare, this was going to be his home. . .at any cost. . .and the outside world finding out about the beasts would make that impossible.

The men who had come out to help stop the monsters charging the shanty town stood their ground as Ben and the others ran into their midst. A cacophony of gunfire thundered. It was deafening. Ben wanted to slap his hands up over his ears and cover them but couldn't without letting go of his AK-47.

A Sasquatch leapt onto the small, makeshift porch of a trailer where a woman with a double barrel shotgun had just emptied her weapon into one of its snarling brothers. The porch couldn't support the thing's massive form, splintering apart from the impact. The Sasquatch and the woman fell amidst the broken pieces of wood that went down with them. She desperately tried to roll away from the monster, out of its reach. The Sasquatch was too fast though, grabbing her. The woman was screaming. Ben saw that she was but couldn't hear her voice over the thundering gunfire and furious roars of the monsters. He watched helplessly as the beast snapped the woman's spine, yanking her torso back towards it with such force and speed that the bone couldn't bend.

A very brave or very stupid fellow hurled himself from the steps of his trailer onto one of the Sasquatch. The large knife in his hand drew blood as he plunged it into the Sasquatch's shoulder. Jerking the blade free, he stabbed the monster again, over and over, until the beast reared up with a roar and flung him from it. The man went rolling across the snowy ground. He was trying to get to his feet as the Sasquatch came at him. An angry kick from the beast tore the man's head from his body and sent it flying away into the night. Blood spraying from the top of his neck where his head had been, the man's body collapsed in front of the Sasquatch.

But not all of the workers were getting slaughtered. Some of those attempting to fight and stop the on rush of monsters won small victories of their own. A woman with a pistol that looked ridiculously big for her to be using, braced the weapon with two hands, as she fired it almost point blank into the face of a Sasquatch that was charging her trailer. The bullet the gun spat entered the Sasquatch's mouth, breaking several of its teeth, then exited through the base of its neck. The Sasquatch died instantly but was carried on by its momentum, crashing into the side of the woman's trailer as she sidestepped its now aimless charge.

Ben had entirely lost sight of Henry and had no idea where the foreman had run to. Coming to a stop in the center of the shanty town, not seeing any of the beasts coming directly at him, Ben took a moment to look around. There was fighting going on everywhere. Not just outside the trailers and RVs but inside of some them too. A few of the Sasquatch had opted to tear into the homes of the men and women who had opted to try to remain out of the battle. There were corpses everywhere.

Ben couldn't even guess at how many of Henry's workers were already dead. The Sasquatch weren't without losses either. Some of the giant beasts lay dead too. It was clear that the beasts were going to win, however. Between having the element of surprise and their sheer strength and speed, the courage or perhaps desperation of the workers wasn't going to be enough to save them.

Realizing that he hadn't seen Deputy Sorrells at all since everything started, his head twisted about to the left and right, eyes searching for any sign of her. Where the hell was she? She should be right here in the heart of hell with him. A Sasquatch that caught sight of him was bounding his way. Ben didn't know whether to run or open fire at the snarling, yellow-eyed beast.

****

Cassie had taken the gig up here in Alaska because of the high pay. It'd seemed like such a great idea. She and Colby needed the money. Being a single mom wasn't easy and Cassie figured if she could just make it through the months on this project, the money would be enough to allow her a year or more of just being a mom. Cassie could stay home and have the time with Colby that she so desperately wanted.

When all the strange things began to happen around the construction site, Cassie hadn't been worried. They weren't her problem. That's what she told herself. During those days, the threat felt more creepy and like a scare tactic than real danger. When people started dying, Cassie wanted to get out but if she had, it would have meant a breach of contract and the loss of most of the money she'd already earned. There was no way in hell she was doing that. It would screw up everything. Her hands were calloused and battered from the hard work Cassie put in and if she was honest with herself, pride was a factor in keeping her from running too. Now, she was regretting not just taking the loss and having gotten the hell out.

Outside the trailer that served as Cassie's temporary home, a full out war between man and monster was raging. There were screams, snarls everywhere when you could hear them above the cacophony of continuous gunfire. Cassie was glad of making the choice not to go out as everything was starting. This wasn't her fight. All she cared about at this point was staying alive and making it home to her son.

Cassie, unlike a lot of the other workers, didn't have any sort of real weapon in her trailer. She hadn't even remotely thought that bringing something like that with her would have been a good idea. In her hand was a kitchen knife. Cassie's knuckles were white from how tightly she gripped it. Sitting on the edge of her bed, the main door to the trailer was locked, as was the door to the bedroom as well. Cassie wasn't kidding herself in thinking that the doors were thick or heavy enough to stop one of the monsters outside if the thing decided it wanted to get inside and come after her. As the things charged into the shanty community, Cassie had caught a glimpse of them through the living room window of her trailer. That scared the crap out of her. Things like the beasts outside weren't supposed to be real. They weren't supposed to exist in the real world. She'd never seen anything like them other than maybe in her nightmares. The beasts moved about on two legs, looking like a horrid cross between an ape and a man. Their eyes glowed in the darkness of the night.

She thought about getting under the bed and hiding there like a frightened child. It took a lot of effort not to. Cassie knew that if she did that though there would be no hope of getting away if one of the beasts made it into the bedroom and found her. She got up from the edge of the bed and started towards the window. Its curtains were drawn but there was no way to do anything more to secure it as everything went to hell. Her trembling hand reached for the curtains as Cassie summoned up the nerve to attempt to peek out at the battle outside. Edging them just ever so slightly aside, Cassie's heart leapt into her throat at what she saw. In the trailer across from her own, belonging to an A hole named Jeb with whom she'd never gotten along with, was a huge hole through its side where one of the beasts appeared to have torn its way in. Jerking her hand away, Cassie let the curtains fall back into place. She'd figured that Jeb was a coward and would stay in his trailer like her. That wasn't a surprise. Seeing that doing so hadn't saved him made Cassie's stomach turn. She had no time to be sick though.

The trailer shook beneath her feet as if something had blown up under it. Cassie lost her balance, falling with a thud onto the bedroom's carpet. Whatever was under the trailer thudded into its bottom again. This time, the floor buckled upstairs, giving way to the force being exerted against it. Cassie found herself staring directly into the burning, yellow eyes of a monster. The musky stink of its hair filled her nostrils, making Cassie gag. She rolled away from the beast. It stood up through the hole it had made in the floor. Cassie screamed despite herself as the beast pulled itself up into the bedroom. The floor creaked and seemed to barely hold together beneath the thing's weight with each massive footfall. It was coming towards her. Cassie, on her feet again, backed into the room's corner. The monster was between her and the room's door. She glanced at the window considering trying to jump out through it. Fighting the monster with just the kitchen knife in her hand would be suicide and Cassie knew it.

Snarling, the giant beast lumbered closer. Cassie watched, her heart pounding against her ribcage. She hoped the floor would give way under its feet but that wasn't happening. Her eyes darted to the door and then back to the window. Cassie knew she had to make a move. The problem was that going for either put her easily within the monster's reach. The choice was taken from her as the monster caught her off guard, lunging forward.

Screaming, Cassie did the only thing she could, slashing at the monster with the kitchen knife. Its blade drew a thin line of blood slicing along the length of the monster's lower, right arm which seemed to only enrage it more. Cassie's screams were silenced as its left hand clasped her head. Oversized fingers obscured her vision and blinding pain shot through her head. She could feel the bone of her skull bulking as the monster yanked her head forward and then just as quickly rammed it backwards. Cassie died as her head was shoved through the wall of the trailer. The beast let go of her corpse, leaving it dangling against the wall, held there by the upper part of her body that was within the wall itself.

****

Ben opened fire with his AK-47 held just above his waist, aimed at the Sasquatch's lower body. He wasn't trying to kill the beast but rather just stop it from reaching him. Getting ripped apart, limb from limb, just wasn't on his agenda for the night. The rifle spat a stream of rounds at the approaching Sasquatch on full auto. The bullets hammered its legs, groin, and lower torso. The barrage likely would have barely given the Sasquatch pause had not its testicles been hit. They popped like melons being struck by sledgehammers. The beast howled, slapping its hands over the wounds between its hair-covered legs, and dropped onto its knees. Not giving it a chance to get up, Ben closed on the creature, emptying the rest of his rifle's magazine directly into the beast's face. The bullets shredded the flesh of its cheeks and blew out an eye but didn't do anywhere near enough damage to finish off the Sasquatch as Ben had hoped. Even so, at least it wasn't getting up to come after him. Whirling about, Ben ran, ejecting the AK-47's spent magazine and slamming a new one home. Deputy Sorrells was still on his mind. He couldn't for the life of him figure out where she was. She was supposed to be protecting Henry's workers and the site.

A Sasquatch burst through the wall of a trailer, tearing out of it right at him. Ben froze, eyes bugging. How the hell had a beast even gotten into a trailer? It was a dumb question for his brain to pose, especially since his brain should have been busy getting his body moving before the Sasquatch got its hands on him. Standing there gawking, Ben saw that he wasn't going to be able to dodge the beast. Thankfully, Deputy Sorrells showed up out of seemingly nowhere to save his arse. The shotgun she was carrying boomed. The Sasquatch staggered as a large chunk of meat was blasted from its back. It turned towards Sorrells as she worked the pump of her weapon, chambering another round. The wound in its back had slowed the beast otherwise Sorrells might not have been able to get off a second shot before it reached her. Her shotgun boomed again. Sorrells had aimed for the monster's throat and hit her target. The soft flesh stood no chance against the heavy slug. Blood exploded outward in bright red splatters. The Sasquatch made a noise, a sickening gargle, and then stumbled backwards. It fell over onto its back in the snow, twisting and jerking about as it died in pain.

"Thanks," Ben managed to squeak, still not

fully recovered from the state of shock he'd been in.

"Move your ass!" Sorrells yelled, motioning for him to follow her.

She ran away from where the battle continued to rage, heading out of the shanty community. Ben followed after her, doing his best to keep up. He quickly saw where she was heading. . .the parking area at the end of the road below the community of trailers and RVs. Sorrells didn't stop until they were at her patrol car.

"Wha. . .why? Why are we here?" Ben said, trying to catch his breath that was coming in ragged gasps. "Shouldn't we be. . .?"

"What?" Sorrells snapped. "Getting our arses handed to us like your people up there?"

Ben couldn't argue that. They pretty much were despite all the money he had dumped into getting ready for the Sasquatch to attack again. Of course, he hadn't expected an entire tribe of the monsters to be showing up.

"The sheriff is on his way," Sorrells told him, pointing south of them. "And you can bet he's bringing the whole department with him."

Ben stared at her, not sure how to respond. They needed the help but getting it in such a manner was going to make things extremely complicated for him, assuming that he survived long enough. That was a problem for the future though.

Looking down the road, he saw the convoy of patrol cars making its way towards the parking area. There were six patrol cars mixed with several civilian pick up trucks. Sorrells wasn't exaggerating. The sheriff really did appear to have brought every bit of manpower he could with him.

The vehicles came speeding into the parking area, slamming on brakes, and skidding to a halt. Men armed with hunting rifles, shotguns, and even some AR-14s leaped out of the pick up beds. The sheriff and his deputies got out their cars. Sheriff Hawk marched straight up to Sorrells.

"Sit rep?" he barked.

"All hell has broken loose up there," Sorrells answered.

"You armed your workers?" Sheriff Hawk spun on him in a righteous fury as Ben took a step back from the taller man.

"If he hadn't," Sorrells cut in, "they would all be dead already."

The sound of gunfire could be heard from the shanty town above them. It was a lot less in volume now but it hadn't fallen completely silent. That meant there were people up there still alive and in the fight.

"Are you telling me all that is because of a

Sasquatch?" a deputy asked.

"No, Andrew," Sorrells shook her head, "I'm telling you all that is because of a fragging tribe of Sasquatch!"

The men who rode up in the beds of the pick up trucks were waiting on Sheriff Hawk to give the word to join the fight above them. They were much closer to being a local militia than being just a hurriedly assembled posse of trigger happy rednecks. The sheriff's deputies mixed among them, helping to keep order.

"Hey!" Sheriff Hawk silenced both Sorrells and the other deputy. "Enough. We've got work to do."

And with that, the sheriff led the charge up the hill towards the makeshift shanty community where the workers lived.

****

"Die, you fragger!" Harry shouted, his hands moving like lightning as his pistols put bullet after bullet into a hulking Sasquatch that had knelt to tear away a chunk of meat from a worker's corpse and start eating it. The beast made the mistake of turning its head around towards the pistoleer after the first round had slammed into the backside of its skull. Harry's bullets ripped at its eyes, nose, and cheeks. A lucky shot, pulping the Sasquatch's right eye in the process, entered its brain through an eye socket. It fell dead, body twitching in fierce death throes atop the snow-covered ground.

Heather and Harry had rallied the remaining workers, except for a handful that were still keeping hidden inside their trailers and RVs. They were holding their ground now too. The workers combined with their squad had outnumbered the hairy monsters from the start. The brutal fury of the beasts along with the element of surprise allowed them to rampage through the construction site in a killing spree of primal violence. Most of the workers were dead but those that remained stood with him and Heather. There were eight men and women, each armed with the shotguns, rifles, or pistols that were the common use self defense weapons for people who lived in the area. The beasts weren't faring much better. The power of modern firearms had taken a toll on their ranks at last. Harry didn't know exactly how many of the things had originally come out of the woods but only nine of them were still alive in the fight.

The cluster of surviving workers, led by Heather and himself, were scattered as the largest of the beasts plowed into their ranks. The massive Sasquatch stood close to ten feet tall. If the others were tanks, then this guy was a fragging M1 Abrams. All of them were pouring fire into the giant but it was just shrugging off the rounds as if they were nothing. A swipe of a set of claws cut a man's head into three pieces. The giant beast spun to grab up another worker and yanked her body apart. She separated along her middle, flesh tearing, intestines flying out like red-slicked purple snakes erupting from the sort of snake nut cans that lame pranksters loved to use. The woman didn't even have time to scream. Flinging her two pieces away in different directions, the raging monster's eyes locked onto Heather as she raised the M4 in her hands at it. The bullets she fired tore a red trail up the front of the monster's chest but even so all they seemed to do was drive it into a more furious state of rage. The giant Sasquatch threw both its hands skyward, getting ready to bring them down on her. Harry knew he had to do something or Heather would be nothing but a bloody smear on the frozen ground.

"Look out!" Harry yelled, shoving Heather aside. His pistols blazed as he emptied them into the giant Sasquatch. Splashes of red flew from the monster's throat where the bullets punched through the softer flesh there. He and Heather had learned that going for the head, eyes, or throat were the best ways to get penetration and do real damage to the monsters. This big guy was no exception to that. The sharp, unexpected pain caught the giant Sasquatch offguard and sent it reeling backwards.

Harry knew it would eventually bleed out from the wounds he'd just inflicted on it but that wasn't going to save him right now. A giant Sasquatch backhanded him. Harry's breath left his body as the side of his ribcage where its huge, hairy fist made contact shattered. The blow sent him flying several feet through the air to crash down onto his back. The world swam before his eyes, his vision blurring, as Harry fought not just to stay conscious but also to breathe. Each breath hurt like hell and he tasted the saltiness of his own blood in his mouth. He tried to get to his feet but the pain was too intense, forcing him to collapse back onto the snow.

From where he lay, Harry watched the battle. Yelling his name in something akin to a berserker rage, Heather went after the giant Sasquatch. She hosed its legs with a barrage of fully automatic fire from her M4 until the weapon clicked empty. The huge beast didn't fall though. A sickening, wet attempt at a roar rose up from its savaged throat. The strangled, gargling cry had barely left its lips as Heather hurled herself up onto its chest, clinging to the thick hair there with one hand as her other withdrew a grenade from a pocket on her vest and rammed it into the beast's open mouth. She leapt away as the grenade detonated. The Sasquatch's head became a splattering mess of blood and brain matter.

Heather landed face down on the snow with a pained grunt but quickly rolled to her feet, yanking out her pistol from the holster on her hip. Harry continued to watch helplessly as she fought to stay alive amid the chaos of the battle. The Sasquatch were overpowering the workers and ending them one by one. Heather took aim and fired her pistol at a Sasquatch that was effortlessly lifting a woman up from the ground with a single hand. The 9mm rounds did nothing to the beast but the flashes and sharp cracks of her pistol drew its attention to her. The beast smashed the woman it was holding into the side of a trailer so hard that metal bent, bones snapped, and blood splattered. Heather fired again, spending the rest of her pistol's magazine trying to hurt the Sasquatch, aiming for its head. Raising an arm, the beast blocked her shots. Instead of doing real damage they merely pounded against thick muscle without penetrating too deeply. The Sasquatch roared and charged her. Heather was in the process of ejecting the pistol's magazine in order to reload but there just wasn't time. Looking up at the snarling beast charging at her, Heather knew she was about to die. . .but. . . a stream of bullets ripped across its face, slashing and shredding its flesh. The Sasquatch howled, lunging sideways.

"You okay?" Ben asked, having run up beside her.

"Frag!" Heather swore, shaking her head in disbelief. "You got here just in time, Mr. Meyer."

"Call me Ben," he barked at her. "Where's Martin?"

Ben flinched before she could answer, remembering exactly what had happened to his best friend. His mind had blocked it out until he'd said Martin's name.

"The idiots you armed mowed him down," Heather reminded him.

"What about the rest of your people?" Ben asked.

"Dead," Heather's eyes were wet though the expression on her face was one of anger. "They're all dead."

"I brought reinforcements," Ben said, lacking anything better to say.

"I see." Heather looked around and saw Deputy Sorrells among the law enforcement officers and civilians running in to join the battle. "Let's give these apes some fragging payback!"

"Here!" a redneck local tossed Heather a pump action shotgun as he sprinted past her.

Heather caught the weapon, a feral smile spreading her lips.

She and Ben advanced into the shanty town

together in the wake of the crowd of rushing officers and armed local men. The few beasts left alive put up a hell of a fight. A Sasquatch met a pair of the men, plunging a hair-covered hand through one and then yanking it free, grabbed the other, snapping him in half over one of its knees. The beast fell though as more men closed in, pouring bullets into it. Most of the remaining beasts were wounded from the battle that had been raging for a while now and that made them easier to kill.

A worker wearing the second of the flamethrowers Ben gave out, emerged from hiding. Who the frag knew where the guy had been since his buddy, carrying the other flamethrower, had died in a horrific explosion. He came at the Sasquatch with a vengeance, hosing two of them. The beasts shrieked as the flames washed over their bodies, engulfing them from head to toe. Flesh cooked and fat boiled as the man with the flamethrower didn't let up.

"Woohoo!" Heather shouted, pumping a fist in the air. "Fry the bastards!"

Soon, the battle was finally over. The dead were everywhere, human and Sasquatch corpses alike littered the snow-covered ground.

****

As the sun came up, Ben was scowling. The

sheriff and two of his deputies, including Sorrells, were all that was left alive out of all the reinforcements who had shown up. Heather, eight of his workers, and himself were the only other survivors. It looked as if they had managed to kill all of the Sasquatch. . . and that made it all worth it to Ben. He could always hire more workers to finish his new home. Martin's death haunted him. The big bodyguard was pretty much his sole friend in life. Still, Ben was used to losing people, though usually it was from him kicking them out of his life once he realized they were there just for the money.

The sheriff, thank God, hadn't argued with him about burning the Sasquatch. On that, they fully agreed. Neither one of them wanted the hassle proof of the beasts' existence would bring. How Sheriff Hawk planned to cover it all up was his problem but he was going to make dang sure he did. It sounded like the story Hawk was going to run with was that there was a fire on the site which led to several explosions killing most of the crew and those who had come to help them. They had talked about it a small bit since he'd promised Sheriff Hawk that every single one of the families of the men and women who had died during the long night would be taken care of for life. Ben had the money to do it and he knew it. Regardless,

Ben assured the proper paperwork would be drawn up after he spoke to his legal team and sent to the sheriff as quickly as possible.

"I can't believe you're still going to build here," Sheriff Hawk frowned.

Deputy Sorrells didn't say anything but she didn't need to. Her expression told Ben that she was just as surprised and confused as the sheriff.

"Of course I am," Ben smirked. "I'm a rather stubborn bastard."

"Well, you can count on me that not a damned soul outside of those here are going to know what really went down," Sheriff Hawk assured him. "And the folks here, they'll be keeping their mouths shut too, as per our agreement."

"I know they will," Ben's smirk became a threatening smile.

"If I were you, I'd hire a new foreman," Deputy Sorrells chimed in. "That guy you got now is one slimy bastard."

"Coward too," Ben nodded. "If he turns up alive, the two of us are certainly going to have a rather intense discussion about how things have gone here."

Sheriff Hawk grunted, "Yeah, you do that."

"Sheriff, Deputy Sorrells," Ben said, "Thank you both for your help."

"It's our job," Deputy Sorrells pointed out.

"We'd have done the same for anyone in trouble. Don't take it personally."

Ben chuckled at that. He knew very well how all the locals, including the two of them, truly felt about him and Sorrells certainly wasn't shy about letting him know her feelings matched theirs. She was one so he couldn't blame her. None of the hicks up here could understand what it was like to have the level of money he did and the woes that came along with it. He needed to get away from the States, away from society, away from the press and media. Ben just wanted a place to call home where he could be alone.

The smell of burning Sasquatch bodies was carried to him on the morning breeze. Ben wrinkled his nose at it. The odor was far from pleasant. The things smelt terrible alive and just as bad in death. Having a flamethrower that survived the battle helped with disposing of the corpses a lot. The worker, Lewis, was at work making sure all of the Sasquatch bodies were reduced to nothing more than ash and bone. Ben had assigned another pair of workers, John and Tyrone, to gather up what was left and make sure it was dealt with according to his instructions. The bones were going to be stored until acid could be brought in to dissolve them. It should be arriving by tomorrow.

Ben walked Sheriff Hawk and Deputy Sorrells to their patrol cars and saw them off. He was glad to be rid of them. Once his people got the contract paperwork to them in regards to what he'd be paying out to the families of those killed at his site then Ben hoped to be done with them forever. There was so much to be done. It felt like he was starting over from nothing. Rationally, Ben knew he wasn't. The ground had already been cleared and was ready for the real construction of his new home to begin but he was going to need a new crew to get it done. With a phone call, he put his people in the States on getting that dealt with too. It wasn't something Ben needed to handle personally.

Heading back to Henry's trailer, he wasn't surprised to see the slimy foreman there waiting for him. The bastard had finally crawled out of wherever he'd been hiding since the battle.

"Thank God," Henry rushed from the trailer's porch to greet him. "I didn't know if you were still alive or not, sir."

"Oh, I made it through the night," Ben quipped. "No thanks to you."

"Sir, I. . ." Henry started.

"You ran away, Henry," Ben stared at the foreman. "I was there, remember? Right next to you. You left me standing there and took off like a bat out of hell."

"I. . .I. .." Henry stammered.

"Henry, let's not make this harder than it has to be. Come on into the trailer with me and we'll talk about what's going to happen from here," Ben's tone made it clear that he meant what he said and the foreman had dang well better do what he said.

"Yes sir," Henry nodded, looking pale and almost frantic with worry.

Ben led the way up the steps into the office home that had belonged to the former since work began on the site. It wasn't going to anymore.

As soon as they were inside the trailer, Ben shut the door behind them and motioned for Henry to take a seat at the desk.

"You're going to fire me, aren't you?" Henry asked, though his voice kept an edge of worry and fear it got surprisingly firmer. "You know that none of this was my fault. Who in the hell could possibly expect to stumble onto real Sasquatch, much less have the things be determined to stop the work you're doing?"

"Heh," Ben's lips twitched in a partial grin. "I can't argue that."

"Good," Henry said, his courage increasing in front of Ben's eyes. "Then you're not going to fire me?"

Ben shook his head. "Why would I do that,

Henry?"

Something in Ben's voice struck Henry wrong. The foreman sat up straight in the seat he'd taken at the desk, eyes locked onto him. It was clear Henry had been expecting the axe to fall on his career. It was true, he had no intention of firing the slime ball. Ben reached into his jacket and pulled out a .44 Magnum.

"Whoa!" Henry shouted, leaping to his feet. "Ben, let's not be crazy!"

Paying him no heed, Ben quickly took aim at Henry and squeezed the Magnum's trigger. The shot caught Henry directly in his sternum, shattering it on the way to his heart. The impact of the bullet tearing into his chest sent Henry reeling backwards. The foreman crashed into the wall behind the desk and slid down it to collapse sprawled out on the trailer floor.

Ben calmly walked over to where Henry lay, checking to ensure that he was dead. No one else, except maybe a few of his surviving workers, knew for sure that Henry had still been alive at the end of the battle. The sheriff and Sorrells didn't. Cleaning up the mess that was Henry would be easy and not a soul would ever truly know what had just happened in this trailer.

All of the problems were finally over now and the work towards his future home could start back.

Ben smiled, placing the pistol back inside his jacket. He left Henry lying in a growing pool of blood and headed back outside. He stepped into the morning air and looked up at the blue sky above.

Ben smiled. Soon. . . very soon. . . this place would be his home.

****

Three months had passed since the battle with the tribe of Sasquatch that had tried to stop the construction of Ben Meyer's home. Sheriff Hawk and Deputy Sorrells sat in their patrol car parked atop a hill that gave them a clear but distant view of the Meyer estate.

"I can't believe that rich bastard actually got it done," Sheriff Hawk shook his head.

"I can," Sorrells chuckled. "He's too stubborn not to have."

The house was nothing short of a massive mansion. No. It was the biggest home either of them had ever seen in real life. Compound was a better word to describe it. The structure was surrounded by an eight foot tall wall topped with curls of barbed wire. If Hawk had to guess, he'd wager the wire was electrified just to make it that much harder to get over.

Anyone who knew Ben Meyer would be crazy to think that there were a lot people living inside the place. The man was a born loner and a selfish prick to boot. Mostly likely the huge amount of space in the compound was allotted to storage for the man's various collections. It was no secret that Meyer had an obsession for collecting books, toys, movie memorabilia, and swords. You could learn that much about him with a simple internet search which would bring up seemingly countless articles about the amount of money he spent on such things. Sure, most of those stories were published in tabloids but the sheer quantity of them meant that there had to be some truth to the matter. Of course, the compound likely held more than just Meyer's beloved collectibles. It had to be set up with back up generators, shelf stable food stuffs, medicines, and everything an apocalypse prepper could dream of. Meyer had the money and staff to make something like that happen so you could almost count on those things being part of the compound.

Hawk had grown a beard since the battle with the Sasquatch and raised his right hand to scratch at it. He looked over at Sorrells. "I'm going to miss you."

"I'm not gone yet," she managed a smile.

"Yeah, but how in the hell am I going to make it without you?" Hawk said.

Sorrells chuckled. "You'll get by just like you

did before I came along."

"The world wasn't quite as scary of a place back then," he pointed out.

There hadn't been a single Sasquatch sighting or evidence that any of the beasts survived the bloody battle at the construction site. The secret of their existence had been kept too, just like Ben Meyer had wanted. Sometimes he wondered just how much money and what lengths Meyer had gone to behind the scenes to ensure that it had. Still, he knew and so did Sorrells. They had lived through it and gone head to head with the snarling monsters. And it changed them both. Sheriff Hawk had not only grown his beard, he had started drinking when he wasn't on the clock too. He was sure to always be sober for his shifts but at night, Hawk was usually sloshed. When he closed his eyes, if he wasn't drunk out of his mind, the snarling, monstrous beasts were there waiting on him. As for Sorrells, she'd held herself together despite the trauma. If anything, she became an even more by the book officer, going about her job with a renewed zeal. That was at least what could be seen on the surface. Hawk knew their encounter with the beasts had affected Sorrells to her core just like it had him. She'd put in for a transfer to Anchorage. You didn't get more urban than that in Alaska. There, Sorrells would be working in a place where it should be impossible to ever encounter a Sasquatch again. It was clear that was the real reason behind her transfer. Hawk hadn't called her out on that and had no plans to. Doing so would only be an awkward mess that likely would accomplish nothing except to destroy what was left of their friendship.

"That's true," Sorrells frowned. "I'd be lying if I told you that I didn't feel kind of guilty leaving you here but. . ."

"I know," Hawk cut her off. "The new gig is just too good to turn down. Hell, I don't blame you there. You'll be making more than anyone here in Higton could ever hope to."

"It's not just the money," Sorrells looked ashamed.

"Sorrells," Hawk said her name softly. "It'll give you a chance to solve some real crimes, make a difference. I get it. I really do."

"Thanks, boss," she met his eyes, almost tearing up. Sitting up fully in the passenger seat to peer out the front window at Meyer's compound, she changed the subject a bit. "I'm glad we came up here to get one last look at this place together. It just feels right that we did. Maybe we'll both get some closure from this."

Sheriff Hawk grunted. "I don't know about that. The place is still in my jurisdiction."

"Sucks to be you," Sorrells punched his shoulder, joking to cut the tension that had grown inside the patrol car.

"What say we get you to the airport?" he asked.

"Sounds good to me," Sorrells smiled.

Sorrells' plane was due to leave in just a few hours and neither of them wanted her to miss it.

Sheriff Hawk put the patrol car into reverse, backing it around so that he could head down the hill towards the main road. The sun had begun its descent in the sky and the shadows among the trees were growing longer and deeper. Sheriff Hawk took one final glance at the Meyer's compound and hoped that as per his word he'd never set foot on the property again.

****

At the center of the section of wall surrounding the Meyer compound facing towards the distant town of Higton, there was a locked iron gate. It wasn't stylish, never meant to be pretty or fashionable. The automated barrier system was built tough enough to stop almost any kind of vehicle from ramming through it. Beyond it lay the road which led up to the door of the main house.

Deep inside the complex, Ben Meyer sat in his study, reading a book. It was an omnibus edition of one of his favourite comics. Since he was little,

Ben enjoyed escaping into another universe of capes and cowls. There, anything was possible. It was so much better than the real world. The best writers knew how to bring the characters on the page to life, breathing into them all the emotions, problems, and romances of real life. Comics were Ben's friends. Unlike any human being he'd ever known, they stuck with him.

Caroline walked into the study. Ben gently closed the omnibus and looked over his desk at her. She was younger than he was by about ten years, making her close to twenty-five. Flaming red hair topped her head and spilled down over Caroline's back and shoulders. She wasn't an athlete but neither was Caroline out of shape. She was a perfect example of what the female form was meant to be to Ben. Green eyes filled with a keen intelligence met his as she spoke in a voice that seemed too deep to belong to such a lithe figure.

"Mr. Meyer," Caroline said, "Will you be requiring anything for the day?"

Ben shook his head. "No. Thank you. Have a goodnight. Caroline. I'll see you in the morning."

Caroline nodded, turning to leave the way she'd come. Ben watched her go, enjoying doing so greatly. Her hips moved in a wonderful rhythm and the entire thing was beautiful. He felt desire stirring within him. Ben almost called Caroline back but didn't, reminding himself that he had other plans for the evening.

As much as Ben preferred to be alone, he was wise enough to know that nothing existed in a vacuum. Even he needed interaction from time to time. Also, his new home, the great sprawling compound he had constructed, was too much for any one person to maintain. Therefore, it was inhabited by three people in addition to himself. Caroline was his personal assistant. . .and more. Heidi was Caroline's opposite in terms of cognitive reasoning and intelligence. The same couldn't be said about her physicality. Both women were equally attractive, just in different ways. Whereas despite her beauty Caroline appeared just as another woman you might bump into on the street of any large, modern city, Heidi was every inch the supermodel one might see in the pages of a fashion magazine. She was blonde, young, and thin with pale skin that gave her an appearance of graceful innocence. In truth, that was the last thing she was. Heidi was employed to "service his needs" and she felt no shame about that. A professional to her core, Heidi lived up to what her resume implied and then some. Ben had certainly never been disappointed in her services. And tonight, it was time for to earn her pay again. For a fleeting moment, Ben thought about calling out to Caroline to see if she might join them but stopped himself. Unlike Heidi, Caroline retained at least some semblance of dignity. He could perhaps attempt to order her to join in but doing so risked driving her away even more. Ben sighed. Not even the amount of money he had could buy everything. And he couldn't risk losing Caroline. She was too fragging good at her job of keeping his home and finances organized to live without.

The fourth and final person living in his new home was Owen, his replacement for his long time bodyguard, Greg Martin. When Martin died, Ben felt like he had taken it worse than he should have. The man had been his only real friend but still, Ben prided himself on being detached from humanity. He knew though that everyone could be replaced. Owen was more than a suitable replacement too. A former soldier like Martin, Owen knew both how to kill and protect. The man wasn't as big and tough seeming as Martin had been but what he lacked in strength and bulk, Owen more than made up for in speed and skill. Owen was a one man security force for the compound. With all the cameras and sensors built into the place, Owen could watch everything going on and even sections of the woods outside without ever leaving the security room. Ben had spared no expense on the arsenal available to Owen and the former soldier greatly appreciated that. The two of them had hit it off from the first moment Owen had walked in for an interview or Ben would never have hired him. Ben didn't entrust his life to just anyone and that was basically what Owen's job was, to keep him safe and alive. In addition to being a hardened veteran, Owen was also a qualified nurse, having gone into that profession after leaving the military, until Caroline reached out to him on Ben's behalf, offering him the gig here at the compound.

Ben spun around in his chair to look out the huge window behind him. Outside, a few flakes of snow were blowing about as the sun was beginning its descent below the mountains that surrounded the compound. It wasn't as late as he thought it was. Glancing at his watch, Ben saw that the time was six forty-seven. Rumbling, his stomach pointedly told him that he needed some dinner. Hiring a cook for the compound was something that Ben had Caroline working on but for now, it was everyone for themselves when it came to food, cooking or having delivered their own. Getting up from his chair, Ben found himself approaching the window rather than heading out in search of food. He stood in front of it, staring not at the blowing snow, but at the wall encircling the compound. Beyond it, he knew, were miles upon miles of woods. Ben sighed again. He vividly recalled the monsters that had lived among those trees which he had been forced to eradicate in order to build his home here. Sometimes he wondered if the losses that came with doing that were worth it. His gaze moved skyward. The dark clouds of a storm were gathering. It looked like it was going to be a bad one. Ben wasn't worried. The house would be fine for quite some time in terms of power, even if the main local grid went down.

****

Owen's feet were propped up atop the console below the dozens of monitors covering the wall he faced. He yawned, mouth opening wide, stretching his arms upwards. The weather outside was turning nasty. Owen hated the cold and snow and they were in for a ton of both. There had been no way he could turn down this job though. He needed the money too badly. When his wife left, Helen took everything with her, right down to their house. The job offer to become a bodyguard and medic for the millionaire, Ben Meyer, came along at the perfect time to save his butt from living on the street. Plus the job was easy peasy. The worst he had dealt with since arriving at the compound were a lost delivery guy, some hunters trespassing on the outskirts of the property, and a fragging bear that left him no choice but to put it down as it was too dangerous to just leave hanging around.

The cameras which were feeding images to the monitors had audio components as well. Owen could hear the wind howling outside through them just as he could see that the final rays of the day's sun were dimming and fading to black. The trees beyond the compound's wall were swaying. Yawning again, he closed his eyes. It would be so easy just to go to sleep. Hell, it wasn't like anything was going to happen if he did.

The sharp crack of a tree trunk breaking caused Owen to almost fall out of his chair. His feet slammed onto the floor as he sat up straight, eyes searching the monitors to see if he could see the tree that must have just collapsed. He spotted it quickly. The tree had fallen on the north side of the compound, not close to the wall, but directly onto it. The barbed wire was torn free and flopped about in the howling wind. The wall itself appeared to be mostly damaged at its top by the tree. The tree was huge. It had to weigh a fragging ton. Still, the wall was standing and not completely crushed and ruptured. That was good. Regardless, the mess was going to have to be fixed as soon as the weather permitted. He'd need to get a professional crew of contractors up here to deal with it. While he might be able to get the tree off the wall by himself, Owen couldn't fix the wire or top of the wall on his own. Owen had somehow managed not to knock the cup of coffee that had been near where his feet were from the top of the console in his moment of panic. He grabbed it now. The liquid in the cup was black and cold. Chugging it down, Owen forced himself to focus on the problem that just landed in his lap. It wasn't an emergency that couldn't wait but he doubted Mr. Meyer was going to be happy about it. Even so, Owen knew he should head out and get a better look at things up close. There was only so much you could tell through a security feed.

Owen stopped by his room first to grab a heavy, hooded jacket. There was no point in freezing his butt off any more than he had to. He didn't hit the armory. It was just a fallen tree and besides, there was never a time he wasn't armed. On his hip was holstered a Glock 20. The Glock 20 used 10 mm rounds not 9 mm like most other Glocks. He wasn't planning on going outside the wall so animals shouldn't be an issue, he thought, remembering his encounter with the bear he'd been forced to kill.

Knowing that Mr. Meyer was either with Heidi or getting ready to see her, Owen didn't dare take the chance of interrupting them. Meyer could be an A hole at the best of times. He sure as hell didn't want to tick off the boss by messing with his nightly stress release. Owen picked up his pace as he raced through the house's winding corridors. He considered contacting Caroline to make her aware of what had happened outside but decided against it. She couldn't really do anything more than he was already.

Finally reaching the door leading out of the compound that was closest to where the tree had come down, Owen stepped outside into the falling snow. The shock of the cold was like a kick in the groin as the wind whipped over him. Owen yanked his parka tighter about himself and then adjusted its hood to better protect his ears. He could see his breath in the frigid air. There wasn't a lot of snow accumulated on the ground yet by Alaskan standards. Owen trudged through it towards the wall where the tree had struck, looking the area over as he drew closer to it.

Owen stopped, staring at the mess in front of him as he realized that the tree was moving. At first, he thought it was the wind but quickly realized that wasn't the case. Something huge pulled itself onto the tree, using it to heave its massive form over the fence. The creature landed on the snow and then stood up like a man would. Fully erect the thing was over eight feet tall. It wore no clothes despite being humanoid. Hair covered the bulk of its body. The rest was exposed scar tissue. Owen felt his lunch trying to come up his throat at the sight of it. The creature looked to have been set on fire at some point. The scar tissue was a worm-ish pink, with a fibrous texture that was almost shiny in some spots. Half of the thing's face was like that and on that side, its eye socket was an empty, hollow void.

Drawing his Glock 20 with the speed of an Old West gunfighter, Owen levelled the barrel of the pistol at the beast.

"Hold it right fragging there!" Owen shouted, handling the beast much like he had the bear, trying to seem larger and more threatening than he was. Meyer had told him about the monsters that supposedly had once lived in the woods around the compound. Owen hadn't believed him. He had thought Meyer was utterly whacko. Sasquatch weren't real. Now, he was staring one of those monsters in the face, its half-burnt, nauseating face.

Owen nearly gagged. The beast smelled as bad as it looked. It stunk of rot, death, and animal musk. He involuntarily backpedaled from the thing.

The scarred beast sprung at him with blinding speed. Owen would never have believed something so huge could move as quickly. His Glock 20 boomed too late. The beast was already upon on, ripping the gun from his grasp, as Owen squeezed the trigger. The Sasquatch's other hand closed around his throat, crushing it. No longer able to breathe, Owen kicked and thrashed as the beast lifted him effortlessly from the ground with a single hand. Seeing that he wasn't going to escape his fate, Owen raised his arms up over the beast's so that he could see the screen of his watch. Desperately he stabbed at it trying to activate the compound's security system. Not knowing whether or not he'd succeed due to his blurring vision, Owen's eyes rolled up to show only whites as its grip grew even tighter about his neck. The last thing he saw was the dark sky above before his soul departed from the material world.

****

The Sasquatch drew Owen's body close, sniffing it. This wasn't the one it was after. The scent of that one was on this corpse though. Dropping the body, it stared at the compound for a moment, getting its bearings. The Sasquatch saw the transparent sections in the structure's walls where there looked to be nothing but were actually thin plates of material that shattered when hit, remembering that from the battle months ago when it entered one of the strange metal dwellings the men lived in as it had smashed through such a thing then. Through one of the transparent panes, it saw a female. Her body was lean but breasts large. She was barely clothed by the standards of those of her kind it had seen previously. The lights inside where she stood had turned red and were flashing now. There was an expression of abject terror in the female's eyes. The Sasquatch realized that she saw it. Rearing its head back to release a thunderous roar, it charged forward. The transparent pane was large enough to come crashing through into the room where the female was. Pieces of glass flew, raining onto the floor. The female was screaming at the top of her lungs. It was a high-pitched shriek that only served to make the Sasquatch angrier than it already was. Grabbing the female, the Sasquatch took hold of her head and with a snapping twist, ripped her head away from her shoulders. Even as the female's corpse toppled over, blood spraying from the stub of her neck, the Sasquatch was bursting through the doorway that led deeper into the compound. Bits of wood exploded outward from the breaking door into the hallway beyond the room as the Sasquatch came through it. Only then did it pause to sniff the air. The scents around it confirmed that this place was indeed the home of the one that had slaughtered its brothers and sisters. . .and that he was still here.

Bounding down the corridor in the direction that the scent was strongest, the Sasquatch moved with incredible speed. Its black lips were parted in a fierce snarl. Rounding a corner, it ran straight into another female. The power of the impact knocked her upwards and into the corridor's wall. There was a crunch of bone as she made contact with it. The Sasquatch didn't stop to see if the female was alive or dead. She didn't matter. Only the murderer it had come after was on its mind.

The Sasquatch came to a stop outside a wooden door that stunk with the scent of the murderer. The men had a language like its own kind did. In it, the murderer was called Meyer. The Sasquatch had heard the word yelled and shouted at the murderer enough during the battle its tribe died in to know that it was his name. It stood there, breathing in heavy pants of rage. The murderer was cunning, perhaps on the other side waiting to strike. There was no other option than to go through the door. If it went back outside and tried to enter this place again from another angle, it might give the one called Meyer a chance to escape its fury. That couldn't be allowed to happen. Steeling itself for whatever evil might await it, the Sasquatch hurled itself at the door. The wood splintered and gave way against its weight. Meyer was waiting on it just as the Sasquatch had thought. The death spitting stick in his hands flashed and thundered. Ignoring the searing pain that coursed through its shoulder, the Sasquatch closed on Meyer. It could see the fear in Meyer's eyes. The man stunk of it too. The odor was like a sweet nectar to the vengeance-driven beast. It had to deal with the death stick and fast. With a swipe of one of its massive hands, the Sasquatch knocked the weapon sideways in Meyer's grasp as its barrel flashed again. This time the death the stick spat blew a hole in the wall of the room instead of its body. Its strike sent the death stick spinning away from Meyer. It clattered to the floor several yards away. Meyer stood, mouth fallen open in shock, gawking at it. The Sasquatch didn't want to kill him quickly. The man deserved to suffer for what he had done.

At the far side of the room part of the wall was composed of rocks. Inside the open space at their center was a blazing fire. If it knew what a smile was and what it meant, the Sasquatch would have smiled now. Meyer staggered backwards trying to get away from it. The Sasquatch reached out and shoved him to the floor then dropped down onto him. Catching one arm then the other, the Sasquatch bit through each at the wrist, severing Meyer's hands from his body. The man was screaming and thrashing vainly about. He was far too weak to break free from its hold. With Meyer's hands dealt with, the Sasquatch went for his feet next, biting through his ankles. Keeping Meyer pressed to the floor with a hand planted upon his chest, the Sasquatch used its other to strip him of his clothes, tearing them off. Its claws drew more blood from Meyer in the process but the Sasquatch was careful to make sure that they didn't slash deeply enough to kill.

"Just fragging kill me already!" the man spat in the Sasquatch's face.

A low, guttural growl rose from it as the Sasquatch got its feet and dragged Meyer towards the fire. It shoved the stump of each of Meyer's limbs into the flames, holding them there long enough to char the flesh at their ends. The man was crying like a baby, tears streaming from his eyes.

The Sasquatch stomped across the room, dragging Meyer with it, one hand gripping his left leg just above where the stump of that ankle smouldered. The man had fallen silent. That was okay. It didn't matter, though it would soon. The Sasquatch smashed the glass of the room's window and stepped through after pausing to lift Meyer into its arms. Carrying the man, it walked towards the wall that surrounded the compound. There was a single tree just inside the wall that hadn't burnt down during the battle months ago. It was the last of the holy trees and the perfect place for the murderer to meet his end.

Lifting Meyer to where his face was level with its own, his body pressed against the tree, the Sasquatch slapped him just enough for the man to return to consciousness. The Sasquatch raised Meyer higher until it was looking at his groin. With a chomp, it bit away all of his man parts. Meyer wailed, thrashing against the tree. Its bark tore at the naked flesh of his back, only adding to his pain. Hot, wet red smeared the hair around the Sasquatch's mouth. It relished every second of Meyer's pain and suffering, drinking it in for as long as it could until seeing that Meyer was on the verge of passing out again. The Sasquatch knew that the time had come to take its final vengeance. It yanked Meyer away from where he was pressed against the tree and then slammed onto one of its limbs. The limb went through the center of Meyer's chest like a spear, impaling him.

The Sasquatch stepped back to appreciate the masterpiece it had created. It stared at Meyer's naked, mangled corpse hanging upon the tree as the falling snow swirled in the air, as if sharing its joy at the man's death. Letting out a series of bark-like grunts, the Sasquatch called out to the woods beyond the wall. At the sound of its deep cries, half a dozen smaller beasts came scampering up the fallen tree and over the wall to enter the compound. They approached the Sasquatch. It looked them over happily, the next generation of its kind. It gestured at Meyer's corpse upon the tree and the young ones descended on it, teeth gnashing and gnawing. When they were done, Meyer's legs and lower body were little more than bone.

The Sasquatch turned away from where Meyer hung, content that justice had been served, and left him there, heading back into the woods beyond the wall. The little beasts followed after it.

Meyer's corpse, frozen and drenched in its own blood, would hang there for weeks before finally being found.

END

ABOUT THE AUTHOR

Eric S Brown is the author of numerous book series including the Bigfoot War series, the Psi-Mechs Inc. series, the Kaiju Apocalypse series (with Jason Cordova), the Crypto-Squad series (with Jason Brannon), the Homeworld series (With Tony Faville and Jason Cordova), the Jack Bunny Bam series, and the A Pack of Wolves series. Some of his stand alone books include Manhunt, Cryptid Park, War of the Worlds plus Blood Guts and Zombies, Casper Alamo (with Jason Brannon), Sasquatch Island, Day of the Sasquatch, Bigfoot, Crashed, World War of the Dead, Last Stand in a Dead Land, Sasquatch Lake, Kaiju Armageddon, Megalodon, Megalodon Apocalypse, Kraken, Alien Battalion, The Last Fleet, and From the Snow They Came to name only a few. His short fiction has been published hundreds of times in the small press in beyond including markets like the Onward Drake and Black Tide Rising anthologies from Baen Books, the Grantville Gazette, the SNAFU Military horror anthology series, and Walmart World magazine. He has done the novelizations for such films as Boggy Creek: The Legend is True (Studio 3 Entertainment) and The Bloody Rage of Bigfoot (Great Lake films). The first book of his Bigfoot War series was adapted into a feature film by Origin Releasing in 2014. Werewolf Massacre at Hell's Gate was the second of his books to be adapted into film in 2015. Major Japanese publisher, Takeshobo, bought the reprint rights to his Kaiju Apocalypse series (with Jason Cordova) and the mass market, Japanese language version was released in late 2017. Ring of Fire Press has released a collected edition of his Monster Society stories (set in the New York Times Best-selling world of Eric Flint's 1632). In addition to his fiction, Eric also writes an award-winning comic book news column entitled "Comics in a Flash" as well a pop culture column for Altered Reality Magazine. Eric lives in North Carolina with his wife and two children where he continues to write tales of the hungry dead, blazing guns, and the things that lurk in the woods.

SEVEREDPRESS

@severedpress
/severedpress

Check out other great

Cryptid Novels!

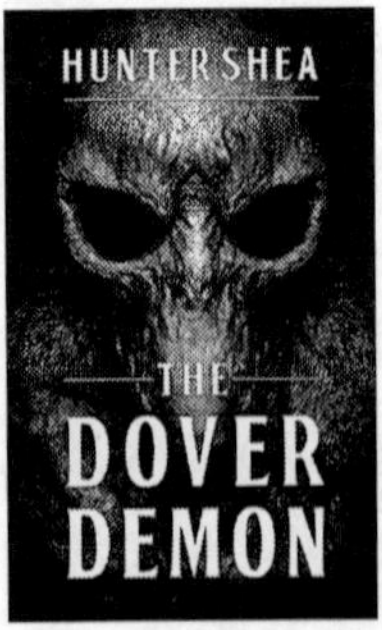

Hunter Shea

THE DOVER DEMON

The Dover Demon is real...and it has returned. In 1977, Sam Brogna and his friends came upon a terrifying, alien creature on a deserted country road. What they witnessed was so bizarre, so chilling, they swore their silence. But their lives were changed forever. Decades later, the town of Dover has been hit by a massive blizzard. Sam's son, Nicky, is drawn to search for the infamous cryptid, only to disappear into the bowels of a secret underground lair. The Dover Demon is far deadlier than anyone could have believed. And there are many of them. Can Sam and his reunited friends rescue Nicky and battle a race of creatures so powerful, so sinister, that history itself has been shaped by their secretive presence? "THE DOVER DEMON is Shea's most delightful and insidiously terrifying monster yet." – Shotgun Logic Reviews "An excellent horror novel and a strong standout in the UFO and cryptid subgenres." –Hellnotes "Non-stop action awaits those brave enough to dive into the small town of Dover, and if you're lucky, you won't see the Demon himself!" – The Scary Reviews PRAISE FOR SWAMP MONSTER MASSACRE "B-horror movie fans rejoice, Hunter Shea is here to bring you the ultimate tale of terror!" – Horror Novel Reviews "A nonstop thrill ride! I couldn't put this book down." – Cedar Hollow Horror Reviews

Armand Rosamilia

THE BEAST

The end of summer, 1986. With only a few days left until the new school year, twins Jeremy and Jack Schaffer are on very different paths. Jeremy is the geek, playing Dungeons & Dragons with friends Kathleen and Randy, while Jack is the jock, getting into trouble with his buddies. And then everything changes when neighbor Mister Higgins is killed by a wild animal in his yard. Was it a bear? There's something big lurking in the woods behind their New Jersey home.Will the police be able to solve the murder before more Middletown residents are ripped apart?

Check out other great

Cryptid Novels!

Edward J. McFadden III

THE CRYPTID CLUB

When cryptozoologist Ash Cohn receives a gold embossed printed invitation inviting him to join The Cryptid Club, he sees the resolution to all his problems.Famous cryptid scientist and biologist, Lester Treemont, one of the world's richest men, and the leader of the Cryptid Club, is dying. What he offers via his invitation is a chance to succeed him. To take over his wealth, laboratory, and discoveries. All Ash has to do is beat eight others like him in a series of tests both mental and physical involving Treemont's collection of cryptids. Seems simple enough, and Ash has nothing to lose.Nine strangers from across the globe, all with reasons for wanting to win. When they start dying one by one, the competition shifts to one of survival. Who among them will rise to the top and reign over The Cryptid Club?

William Meikle

INFESTATION

It was supposed to be a simple mission. A suspected Russian spy boat is in trouble in Canadian waters. Investigate and report are the orders. But when Captain John Banks and his squad arrive, it is to find an empty vessel, and a scene of bloody mayhem. Soon they are in a fight for their lives, for there are things in the icy seas off Baffin Island, scuttling, hungry things with a taste for human flesh. They are swarming. And they are growing. "Scotland's best Horror writer" - Ginger Nuts of Horror "The premier storyteller of our time." - Famous Monsters of Filmland

Printed in Great Britain
by Amazon

61639359R00078